THE MIST IN THE MIRROR

THE MIST IN THE MIRROR

Susan Hill

SINCLAIR-STEVENSON

First published in Great Britain
by Sinclair-Stevenson
7/8 Kendrick Mews
London sw7 3hg

A CIP catalogue record for this book
is available from the British Library

isbn 1 85619 167 2

Phototypeset by Intype, London

Printed and bound in England
by Clays Ltd, St Ives Plc

PREFACE

to Sir James Monmouth's

manuscript

London, and the library of my club, towards the end of an afternoon in late November, that bleak, dispiriting time of year when the golden Indian summer days that lingered on through October seem long gone, and it is yet too early to feel the approaching cheer of Christmas.

Outside in the streets the air was raw and a light mizzle greased the pavements, and had chilled my face and damped the sleeves of my coat.

But I had made the best of my walk down through the narrow streets and alleys of Covent Garden, dodging between stalls and barrows, glimpsing the interior of the Halls, lit like glowing treasure caverns within, and so coming briskly towards Pall Mall.

And now, I paused at the doorway of that handsome room, and for a few seconds looked with quiet appreciation on the welcoming, untroubled scene.

The lamps were lit, and a good fire crackled in the great stone fireplace. There was a discreet chink of china, the brightness of silver teapot and muffin cover, the comforting smell mingled of steaming hot water, toast and a little sweet tobacco.

The dreech weather had drawn in a few more than usual

at this time of day but I saw no close acquaintance and I had a mind to drink a quiet pot of tea and glance at the early edition of the evening paper, content in my own company. Nevertheless, I responded readily enough to the nod of the man seated a little apart across the room in one of the deep recesses between reading desks, for he always cut a melancholy figure and my conscience was pricked by seeing him alone.

'Sir James . . .' I sank into the depths of the old mahogany leather. Behind us, the heavy curtains were still undrawn and I could see the street lamps haloed in the thin mist.

'The fag end of a pretty miserable day.'

Sir James Monmouth nodded. He was a reserved, still handsome man, neatly tucked into himself. A lawyer? A civil servant? I had no idea, but he always made himself agreeable to the younger Members in a modest, unobtrusive way, and what I knew of him, I liked.

'Still,' I said cheerfully, as the tea arrived, and I spied the jar of anchovy paste beside the buttered toast, 'I had an excellent walk. I confess to loving the streets of London no matter the weather.'

'Ah,' Sir James said reflectively, 'the London streets. Yes. A man may walk for many an hour through them.' He settled more deeply into his armchair, leaning back so that his face was in shadow.

'Of course, it is a fine thing so long as one has a refuge such as this at the end of an afternoon – lights, a good fire, congenial company . . . tea and toast.'

'Yes,' he replied, after a pause, 'a refuge indeed. I have been glad to find it so.'

'You are generally here, Sir James.'

'Yes. Yes, generally here. I pray I may always be so, for this place is home to me now, and friends and family too.'

Something in his tone affected me, so that I felt a sudden unease, and, rather too heartily, pressed him to have a slice of the excellent toast. But he waved it politely away and, at the same moment, a couple of my friends entered and came across to join us, and the mood was lifted.

'We have been hearing from Sideham,' – Sideham was the Senior Porter – 'about an apparent sighting of a guest wing ghost!'

'I had no idea there was such a thing,' I said. 'A headless guardsman?'

Ffoulkes snorted with laughter, and at once heads were turned in our direction, there was some reproving clicking of tongues, and we became chastened and quiet, and the library settled back into its customary hush.

But the subject of ghosts was raised again as we sat in the smoking room after dinner and, over glasses and pipes, speculated on various theories and philosophies to do with spectres, the afterlife and worlds beyond the grave. The story of the Club Ghost was told – and reckoned to be a feeble and unremarkable one. And though we encouraged one another mildly, trying to set the mood, no good and gripping original tale was produced by any of us.

'There's many an excellent ghost story printed,' Ffoulkes said at last, 'we had better leave the telling of them to the professionals.'

And so the subject dropped, and we went on to talk of quite other matters.

The party broke up just before midnight, and I was crossing the hall towards the cloakroom when I turned, hearing a step immediately behind me.

'You are taking a cab, I daresay?' Sir James Monmouth spoke with a certain diffidence and hesitation.

'No, no. It is but half a mile to my rooms. I shall walk.'

'Then – if I may keep you company for a short step?'

'By all means. Like me, you feel the need of a breath of air before turning in.'

[3]

He did not reply, only went to wait beside the entrance doors. I was quick to don my coat, and we left together.

There was still the same chill mist, which caught the back of the throat and bore city smoke and London's river mingled on its breath.

On the corner, the chestnut brazier glowed faintly, though the seller had packed up and gone an hour or more since.

None were about. The tall, stuccoed buildings loomed, blank-eyed, above us.

For a moment or two we walked without speaking, but I was sure Sir James had not, in fact, come out with me simply in order to stretch his legs after an evening seated indoors. His very silence had a tension about it.

We reached the next corner where a solitary cab waited under the lamp.

My companion stopped.

'I will drop back now.'

'Well, then, I will bid you goodnight, Sir James.'

'A moment . . .' He hesitated. His beak-nosed face was gaunt, and skull-like beneath the thin hair. I realised that he was much older than I had supposed.

'I could not help but overhear, after dinner . . . your conversation in the smoking room.'

'Oh, that was idle enough talk. They are amiable fellows.'

'But you yourself appeared – more serious.'

'I confess that the subject has always held an interest for me.'

'You – believe?'

'Believe? Oh, as to that . . .' I made a dismissive gesture. The topic was not one I wanted to raise again, in that late, silent street.

'I have . . . a story. It is in my possession . . . which perhaps you might care to read.'

'A true story? Or a fiction? You are an author, Sir James?'

'No, no. It is merely an account of certain – events.'

He lightened his tone abruptly. 'At least, it may pass an idle hour, when next you have one.'

Just then footsteps began to be heard, at the far end of the street. Sir James turned his head quickly, and peered through the murk. Then, abruptly, his hand shot out and he clutched my arm. 'I beg you,' he said in a low, urgent voice, '*read it!*'

The clocks of London began to chime the hour.

It was several days before I was at the club again. Business matters took me north and from there I went directly home to Norfolk, where I relaxed by my own fireside, surrounded by my loving, happy family. Young Giles had a new labrador pup which diverted us all a good deal, and Ann was patiently walking Eliza, who was barely three, up and down the yard and across the paddock on her Shetland pony. I had an excellent day's shooting in the foulest weather and returned home with a decent bag, and muddy breeches, happy as a lark.

I never found it easy to make the transition between Foldingay and my quasi-bachelor existence in Town; for an evening or half a day I felt ill at ease, with a foot in each camp and my mind in neither, and I generally called in at the club for a couple of hours to help ease me back.

It was near to nine on that Monday evening when I came in through the swing doors, to be greeted by Sideham.

'One moment if you please, sir, I have a package for you entrusted to my keeping.'

'From the Registered post?' I was surprised. I receive little mail at the club as a rule, save the usual circulars.

'No, sir, it was given to me by Sir James Monmouth.'

'Ah yes.'

Our conversation, and Monmouth's curious behaviour that night, came clearly back to mind – though I had completely forgotten it in the time between. I recalled the empty, silent street and his abrupt change of demeanour, the panic, the fear – I was not sure exactly what it had been, in his eyes and voice.

'I wonder he did not give it to me himself,' I said, as Sideham handed over a packet securely wrapped in brown paper and string.

'Sir James has gone away for a few days, sir.'

I was surprised. The old man was, as he had said to me, 'generally here', ensconced in one corner or other of the place. But perhaps he felt the need for an occasional change of scene, and I thought no more about the matter, only put the packet with my coat and went in to enjoy a whisky and soda.

I spoke to no one, and after a browse through a pile of sporting periodicals, my eyes felt heavy enough to prompt me to think of making for the set of rooms off Piccadilly that answered for home. On the way out, I picked up Sir James's parcel, but had no thought of so much as opening the wrappings that night. I think I had a vague notion that I would take it down to the country with me the following Friday.

But the walk through a very cold night, under a sky bright with stars, stirred me fully awake again, and having nothing else better to do, and not wanting to turn in, only to be tossing for hours in bed, I decided to glance at the first pages of what turned out to be a trio of quarto-sized notebooks, bound in plain black leather. The manuscript was hand-written in a neat, elegant script, as easily legible, once my eye became familiar with it, as any printed book.

I settled into my chair, turning off all the lights save for one, shaded lamp beside me. I suppose that I intended to read for an hour at most, expecting drowsiness to overtake me again, but I became so engrossed in the story that unfolded before me that I rapidly forgot all thought of the time, or my present surroundings.

A bleak London dawn, seeping in around the edges of the curtains, found me still in my armchair, the finished manuscript fallen into my lap, and I into a fitful, dream-haunted, uneasy sleep.

Sir James Monmouth's Story

CHAPTER ONE

Rain, rain all day, all evening, all night, pouring autumn rain. Out in the country, over field and fen and moorland, sweet-smelling rain, borne on the wind. Rain in London, rolling along gutters, gurgling down drains. Street lamps blurred by rain. A policeman walking by in a cape, rain gleaming silver on its shoulders. Rain bouncing on roofs and pavements, soft rain falling secretly in woodland and on dark heath. Rain on London's river, and slanting among the sheds, wharves and quays. Rain on suburban gardens, dense with laurel and rhododendron. Rain from north to south and from east to west, as though it had never rained until now, and now might never stop.

Rain on all the silent streets and squares, alleys and courts, gardens and churchyards and stone steps and nooks and crannies of the city.

Rain. London. The back end of the year.

But to me it was delightful and infinitely strange. There had been no such rain in Africa, India, the Far East, those countries in which I had spent as much of my life as I could remember. There had been only heat and dryness for month after month, followed abruptly by monsoon, when the sky gathered and then burst like a boil and sheets of rain deluged the earth, turning it to mud, roaring like a yellow river, hot, thunderous rain that made the air sweat and steam. Rain that beat down upon the world like a mad thing and then ceased, leaving only debris in its wake.

I had heard occasional visitors from England speak of this blessed, steady, gentle rain, and at such times, a faint half-memory, like the shadow left by a dream, stirred, and came almost to the surface of my consciousness, before drifting out of reach again. And now I was here, alone in that London rain, in the autumn of my fortieth year.

My ship had docked earlier that day. My fellow passengers had crowded to the rail to watch our progress towards land and the first sight of those loved ones who awaited them. But I, who knew no one, and had no friends or family to greet me, had stayed back, half curious, half afraid, and full of a sudden fondness for the ship that had been my home for the past weeks. For I had no other now. The east was behind me, my life there over. Although I had certain vague plans, and a task I had more or less set myself, the future, and this England, were unknown.

The ship's siren boomed, and was answered from onshore. Hats went up into the air.

I turned then and gazed back down the long dark ribbon of London's river that led away to sea, and felt for that moment utterly dejected, and as bleak-spirited and lonely as I had felt in my life.

My story up to that date may be told briefly enough. I knew only that I had been sent abroad from England when I was five years old, after the death of my parents, of whom I had no recollection at all, and about whom I knew nothing.

My past memories were all of life as a young boy in Africa, with the man who was my Guardian, and called so by me. He told me that he had been an old friend of my mother's family, no more, and until his own death, when I was seventeen, he never spoke to me at all about my birth, early upbringing, home or family. Those places and people, those first years of my life, might never have been, and such faint memories as I had of them I must quickly have learned to suppress for my own peace of mind – and so they became quite buried.

Whether I had been happy or unhappy, *what* I had been before, I also did not know. Only in dreams, sometimes, or those odd, fleeting moments of half-awareness, did I catch a fragment of some mood, some inner sense or feeling or vision – I am uncertain what to call it – which I assumed, because it bore no relation to anything in my present life or the world now about me, must be related to those early years of my life in England.

My Guardian was at that time living in the hills of Northern Kenya, and it is from there that my first conscious memories date. We lived in a roomy, airy bungalow on a farm, and I went to an elementary school in the town twenty miles away. The education I received there was less than adequate, though I think that I enjoyed my days well enough. My Guardian possessed a good, solid, middlebrow library which I had the run of, and it was through this that I made up for many of the gaps in my school learning.

But, although I found some solace and company in books, I was at heart an outdoor boy, living a life in the open air for as much of the time as I could manage, running half-wild, taking in all the sights and sounds and glories of that most liberating and beautiful country.

From Kenya, after some years, we went to India, and thence to Ceylon, where it was proposed that I learn the tea trade. But I found the idea of travelling further, to remote and romantic places, more to my taste than the prospect of settling down to any sort of career, and secretly, I began to plan for myself the life of a nomad, full of exploration and adventure. I had read in particular about the journeys and work of a man I came to regard as one of the greatest of all pioneering travellers. His name was Conrad Vane. I began to pore over piles of maps, books and charts, in the evenings, planning my own future journeys.

When I was seventeen years old, my Guardian was taken very suddenly ill, and, as is the way with many a man who contracts one of the dreadful fevers and agues that strike without warning in those countries, went from robust health to the point of death, in barely twenty-four hours.

I could not pretend to have loved him deeply. But, although he was a reserved, somewhat sombre man, for ten years he had been the nearest to a father I had had. I respected him, liked him, though we were never especially close, and I had never confided to him any of the secrets of my innermost heart and mind.

But to stand at his bedside in the close, steamy air of the bungalow and see his face a dreadful, waxen colour, gleaming with sweat, the flesh already somehow shrunk back, to outline more clearly the skull beneath, shocked and distressed me greatly. I was trying to frame some words of affection but the sentences would not form, and when I next looked down at him, his eyes were staring up at me blankly. He was dead.

For the next twenty years I had travelled, in India and all over Africa, to Burma, Singapore, Malaya, and finally in the remotest areas of China. At first, my travelling had been more or less without purpose, but soon, I had begun to fulfil my ambition of following in the footsteps of Conrad Vane. As I journeyed, I educated myself, by talking to any man I encountered, by living native, and by keeping my eyes and ears open. I also read whatever I could in the history and literature, lore and legends of those countries, and I picked up enough of several languages to serve me reasonably well. I belonged everywhere and nowhere, I was a nomad, and I was always, in the truest sense, alone.

It was a strange, exciting, satisfying life. But it came to an abrupt end when I contracted a debilitating illness in Penang and, during the course of many long, weary weeks, had come to realise that I was finally done with travelling from place to place, I was a middle-aged man and had seen everything I had ever planned to see, and above all, had undertaken virtually every journey Vane himself had made. Indeed, so carefully and closely had I followed in his footsteps, some twenty-odd years after his death, that at times I identified with him, felt myself almost to *be* Vane.

In those two score years, I had occasionally met people from England, and had listened intently to their talk about it. Now, I conceived a longing to go back there (for I knew, what my Guardian had briefly told me, that I was an Englishman born and that had been my early home). I did not formulate any definite plans, had no idea where I might settle when I arrived. I had money, held in trust for me by my Guardian and passed to me on his death, along with such funds and belongings as he himself had had, and I had lived frugally, these past years; there was more than enough to pay for my passage, and bring me in a modest income. Above all, I wanted to discover more about the early life of Conrad Vane, before he had embarked on his travels and begun to write about them – for he, too, had been an exiled Englishman – and I had some idea of paying my eventual tribute to him in a book. I felt that he and his work had been neglected, and was now in danger of being entirely forgotten.

When I was strong enough, therefore, I sold most of my possessions, packed up the rest – there was precious little to show for the past twenty years – and booked my passage.

And now, here I was, alone in the London rain, on that drear and melancholy night.

The bulk of my belongings were to be stored at the dock, and I carried only an old canvas grip containing enough to see me through a day or so. I planned to find rooms as quickly as I could, so that I might lodge in London until I had my bearings, and could see my way ahead more clearly. For now, I obtained from the shipping company offices a couple of addresses of inns at which I might put up. At first, they had assumed that I would want to stay in one of the smarter areas of the city, but I had indicated that I would feel more comfortable in some plain, workaday place close by the river. I was not accustomed to fancy furniture and feather beds. After discussion between themselves, the clerks had decided on names, and warned me against picking out any other places for myself, en route. I rejected all suggestions of a porter to accompany me, and, armed with my bag and the slip of paper, walked out from the warehouses and sheds, through some great gates, and found myself at once in a warren of narrow streets.

It was early afternoon but already the light was fading and darkness drawing in. A chill wind sneaked down alleyways and passages off the river. The houses were grimy, shiny and black-roofed with rain, mean and poor and ugly, and regularly interspersed with more, looming, sheds. The air was filled with the hooting of tugs and a plaintive siren, and there was the constant thump of boxes onto the wharves.

Few were about, though here and there, in half-open doorways and up dark snickets, I glimpsed a solitary figure, or a huddle of ragged children. Once or twice only, a cab went by, but at a great rate, as if anxious to be clear of these particular streets.

But although it was grim enough and cold and damp too, I had begun to feel immensely cheerful, and unworried. I had been alone in far shadier backstreets than these, in the cities of the east, and besides, the very act of walking freely after the weeks of being confined on board ship was a pleasure enough.

A couple of times I passed rough-looking public houses and a glance inside revealed to me the sort of places the shipping company clerks had warned me away from, but at this time of day, there were few drinkers, and the rooms looked uninviting enough in the sour light.

After taking some wrong turnings and having to retrace my steps, I came upon Keypack Hythe Street and, almost by accident, the door of the Cross Keys. By now, the rain had eased to a light drizzle, and there was a sudden parting in the clouds to let through a last few watery rays of sun, which flared briefly onto the narrow windows. I stopped and set down my bag. Ahead of me, under the painted inn sign, was a heavy wooden door, with a latch, reached down half a dozen worn steps from the street.

I turned, and looked about me. To the east, where the sky was dark, the black lines of the warehouses were almost blotted out. To the west, at my back, the blood-red streaks of cloud and the setting sun. I felt inquisitive, keyed up with the interest and excitement that foreign surroundings always induced in me, and in a sense I felt at home too, for although this was a new, colder air than I was used to, there is something familiar about any port to a seasoned traveller – the sights, smells, activities, even the sprawl of streets and wharves that surround and owe their existence and livelihood to it. I was merely used to a closer, steamier air, and to the stink of the east.

As I stood, getting my bearings, studying the houses about me, my eye was caught by some slight movement at the corner, and I glimpsed a figure. It seemed to be that of a boy, some twelve or thirteen years old, thin, with a pale face above a dirty, collarless shirt. For a second, no more, I saw him look full at me, and then past me quickly, as if anxious or afraid to meet my eye. But then I saw that the sun, having flared up again suddenly against the windows, was the next second extinguished, snuffed out like a candle, as it set behind streaked storm clouds. When I looked back, the boy was gone, I supposed disappeared up the slit between the houses, and the narrow street was in darkness.

[15]

CHAPTER TWO

I turned and descended the flight of shallow, worn stone steps, and, pushing open a heavy oak door which had been left ajar, entered the Cross Keys Inn.

For a few seconds, until my eyes grew accustomed to the gloom, I could see nothing. The hallway was cold and had a dank, below-ground smell, mingled with the fumes of smoke and ale, which must have permeated those walls over scores, perhaps hundreds, of years, for this was clearly an immensely old house.

I stood still, expecting to hear voices, or have someone appear. There was nothing. All was dark and silent, save for, somewhere within, the heavy ticking of a grandfather clock.

And then, without warning, there came a sudden terrible cry – a screech or scream, like the cackle of a crone, or the caterwaul of some creature in its death throes. It came once, ripping into the quiet building, and then twice more, a dreadful noise that made me start forward, and set my heart racing, as I looked wildly about me. A great fear rose from somewhere deep inside me. The noise had awakened terrors, and dim formless memories, though I neither recognised nor recalled the sound.

And then, there was silence again, and only the awful recollection of it was left hanging upon the air.

As I was now a little used to the gloom of the hallway, I saw that another door, also ajar, stood to my left. It took me, down a single step, into a small, dim bar parlour, with a long mahogany counter and a few benches and stools set about. The windows were small and let in scarcely any light. The room was quite empty and I was about to reach for the small brass bell that stood on the bar top, when, glancing upwards, I saw, swinging in a great oval brass cage, the source of those appalling cries. A parrot, with dull green, mouldy-looking feathers and a dreadful hook of a beak, sat there, perched on one leg on its rail. Its eye glittered and it stared steadily, malevolently, straight at me.

I felt my blood run cold. I had encountered plenty of weirder, more exotic and, indeed, more hideous and threatening birds – and, for that matter, beasts too – in my travels. There was nothing especially sinister about what I could see quite well was a perfectly ordinary parrot. And yet I recoiled from it, averted my eyes and stepped involuntarily back. I feared it. Something within me had arisen like a wave of horrible sickness at the sight of it. And far, far at the back of my mind was some forgotten memory, I supposed from remotest childhood, fluttering about like a moth, pattering at the door of consciousness. What was it? Where had I seen such a bird, heard such a cry, and why did it so terrify me? I did not know, could not tell. I only stood there, my hand frozen above the bell, the sweat now sliding down inside my collar, aware only of the black, shining eye and the gently swaying perch of that evil bird.

I was rescued by the entrance of a man, who appeared, ducking low beneath the doorway that led to the regions behind the bar, a hook-nosed, heavy-jowled fellow, wearing a baize apron. But he was civil enough and readily agreed to give me a room and supper for a couple of nights – longer, should I require it.

[17]

'Though you'll be moving on,' he said, 'soon enough.'

'My plans are not yet certain. I want to get the measure of London. I have been in foreign countries for very many years.'

He only nodded, having, apparently, little interest in me or my history, and then led me back through the hall, up two flights of steep narrow stairs and down a passage, to the back of the house, volunteering no remark on the way save a terse warning to mind my head.

The room he showed me into was small and dark, in keeping with the rest of the place, but clean and decently furnished, with a bed, and oak table, and chair. Its window appeared to look down into some inner yard and ahead, over rooftops and chimney pots, scarcely visible now that the last light was filtering out of the sky in a thin livid line to the west.

I unpacked my few clothes and belongings and then I was overcome, all within a few moments, by an exhaustion so profound that my head swam, and my limbs felt heavy and began to ache, and, lying fully clothed upon the bed, I fell at once into as deep a sleep as I think I have ever known. The change of air, the new sights and sounds, relief at having completed the voyage and finally reached my home shores, and perhaps most of all, the intense emotions that had chased one another through me in the past few hours, all had combined to drain me completely of any energy. I was unconscious to myself and to the world for upwards of four hours, and only awakened by a knocking that brought me first through the black lower depths of sleep and up to where strange forms and figures, tattered fragments of dreams, floated about in a greenish twilight, and thence abruptly to the surface.

The room was in total darkness and I lay for several seconds, confused, uncertain where I was or what day or time it might be, my head as heavy as if I had been drugged.

The banging came again and then I located it and myself too, and got up to open the door.

A young woman stood in the narrow passageway outside and, in the wavering light behind her, I glimpsed a second figure, and took a step back to let them in. But when the girl stepped into the room, carrying a jug of hot water and a basin, and went with a slow, lumbering deliberation to place it on the chest, I glanced back and saw that I had been mistaken, and that the passage was empty.

'If you'll want supper, you must go down. We don't serve the rooms.'

She had a plump, bovine face, expressionless save for a film of weariness or boredom overlaying it, and a slow manner of speaking. But as she reached the door, on her way out, she looked briefly at me and the faintest flicker of interest or curiosity passed across her dull eyes, prompting me to ask if there were any other visitors staying in the house that night.

She stopped. 'We only have two rooms. Not many come.'

'Yes. It seems very quiet.'

'Mostly. The rowdy ones go elsewhere.'

'You mean the seamen?'

'We keep a respectable house.'

'Then you live here?'

'With father.'

As she turned into the passage, I said, scarcely knowing why, 'And the boy?'

For I was suddenly sure that there *had* been someone behind her as she entered, and that it had been a boy, possibly the one I had glimpsed in the street, on my arrival – though why he interested me, I could not have told.

'There ain't no boy here.'

'I thought you might have a brother – or the pot boy? I saw one in the street as I came.'

'Oh, out there.' She sounded almost scornful. 'There'd be anyone out there. Boys or the like. Anyone.'

[19]

When she had gone, I went to the window. The rain had stopped. But I could see nothing at all save the feeble light from some room below that scarcely penetrated the gloomy area of the yard. The place seemed to belong to another time and a past far beyond that in which I had been living. Here, I was inhabiting a city of the books and stories I had read as a boy, a place of the imagination rather than any reality, and one which had remained scarcely changed for centuries. For the time being, until I had my bearings, that suited me well. I thought that I would make the transition from my own past and very different life, to whatever future I was to have, quite gradually. Here, in this quiet, dark little inn hard by the river, I had an odd sense of being suspended in a limbo, of belonging to no real time or place.

My room was small and close, and comfortable enough, but there was nothing in it to which I could become attached nor would the people I had so far seen make any claims upon me or, in all probability, impress themselves greatly upon my consciousness at all. I had never yet made any ties or set down roots. In the whole of my adult life I had belonged to no one person or place, since the death of my Guardian so many years before – and of the time before that, of course, I knew nothing.

Whether I would ever do so, I had no idea. But I knew that I had come to the end of travelling, and I was very conscious of my approaching middle years, and aware that, sooner or later, I would have to settle, to make some commitment to a place, and to particular people, or else I should end my life at last, as an isolated, peculiar, unhappy old man.

I washed, and made my way along the dim passages and down the stairs to the bar, where I was served a plain, decent supper in a corner, away from the few drinkers who had begun to drift in and talk together. I would have been content and unperturbed – I was still heavy and a little dazed after my sleep – were I not made to feel thoroughly uneasy and distracted by the steady, malevolent gaze of the parrot, which sat hunched in its brass cage, staring in my direction, and never once turning its head but only half closing its eyelids from time to time, to veil the gleam for a moment, before it glared at me again.

I took a single glass of brandy, still alone at the small table, and then returned to my room. My going attracted as little interest as my presence had done.

In spite of the afternoon's rest, I felt exhausted again, and although I had one of Conrad Vane's travel diaries, of a journey to the Antipodes, and intended to begin re-reading it, the print soon swam before my eyes, and I turned down the lamp and went to sleep.

But, this time, I did not dive so deep into unconsciousness and, when I awoke, I knew at once both who and where I was and, moreover, sensed that only an hour or so had passed. And indeed, when I turned up the lamp, my watch showed that it was not yet midnight. I was now so wide awake, and full of a sudden restless energy, a desire for fresh air and movement, that I dressed and went back downstairs.

The bar was empty and the dreadful parrot cage covered over with a maroon shawl, but the landlord was still about, clearing pots, and he agreed curtly to leave the front door unlatched – I was to shoot the bolts and bar it on my return.

I suppose I intended to walk for perhaps half an hour. I re-traced the route by which I had come here earlier in the day and before long, by cutting down this and that alleyway between the high buildings, came to the River Thames.

The thick rain clouds had completely blown away during the evening and the temperature had dropped a little, so that the sky was clear and showed a multitude of stars. The moon was three quarters full, riding high like another ship over the water and giving enough pale light to see by. I stood and, for a moment, closed my eyes and breathed in the river smell, its sourness and dampness, the pungent mixture of rotted wood and oil and tar, the faint fish stench, and, mingled with it, the distant smell of the open sea. A boat or two slipped secretly down the dark water, lamps bobbing astern, and then another came close to the bank, creaking as it passed me. Farther to my right, the great ships loomed up, somewhere among them the one upon which I had travelled. But I had no yearning to return with them when they sailed away again, no feeling of nostalgia for any of those countries I had left behind. A curious sense of belonging here, of having come home, had settled upon me, so that the smell of London's river seemed a welcome, and even an old familiar, one.

I spent some time walking alongside the wide, flowing water, and then turned away and into a maze of streets and yards and passages and squares that led me towards the city. I felt a strange excitement, as keen as any I had known in my youth, when first arriving in some new land, a desire to see, to know, to discover.

Beside the river it had been quiet, save for the silky sound of the craft through the water and their gentle wash against the bank. I had scarcely seen another person. But now, although at first the streets seemed deserted, I became gradually aware of a hidden life on all sides of me, of figures huddled on steps and in doorways, of footsteps and of sudden hissing, whispering voices. Once or twice a cab passed me, once I caught sight of a constable a little way ahead.

Then I turned again and found myself beside a church, and, hard by it, another, whose spires and roofs were silver as fish scales in the moonlight, and below them, behind locked iron gates, graveyards and vaults, casting long shadows. But they were places of great beauty to me, they held no horror or dread, and I gazed at them in wonder, for these were the very places of which I had read and dreamed, these ancient, graceful London churches.

I passed between tall, narrow, shuttered buildings, the daytime offices of bankers, lawyers, merchants, and, cutting through more alleyways, came upon handsome squares, and gardens in their midst, and, shortly after, a foetid area of yards and tenements and pawnbrokers and little greasy shops, and now there were people, like creatures scuttling through undergrowth, muffled figures, who did not glance up or show their faces, but only vanished quickly, out of sight and earshot.

I should have felt uneasy or afraid, so strange was it all, and so entirely alone was I, but I did not, I felt alert, my mind keen and sharp, crackling with intense awareness. I had the odd sensation that I was following after someone, or that I was in quest of something, and very close to finding it, around the next corner, or the next. I walked well and steadily, my limbs easy, and it was only when I came out upon a broad road that seemed to be leading away from the more densely packed streets of dwellings, that I stopped and came back to a measure of sense. A hundred yards or so ahead of me stood a great, black railway arch, and beyond that, there seemed to be higher, more open ground.

I was lost. I had wandered and wound my way far from the river, and the Cross Keys Inn, probably by several miles.

I stood beside the entrance to a grand, stuccoed mansion, gathering my wits and wondering what best I might do when, catching some slight movement a yard or two behind me, I turned and, again, glimpsed the figure of the boy. He had been following me then, I was quite sure; I saw his face, his dark, anxious eyes and thin neck that protruded above the collarless shirt. He looked at me, and yet once again, somehow into the distance, too, over my shoulder.

Well, I resolved, if he had followed me here, for whatever reason, he could lead me back, and I took a firm step in his direction, half raised my hand to stay him. At that moment, a railway train came roaring across the bridge in a great clatter and belch of smoke and livid flame, sparks showering upwards from its funnel, the men, silhouetted within the cabin, backs bent, black as pitch. It was a magnificent, exhilarating sight, and I spun round to gaze at it with all the astonishment and wonder of a child. The engine seemed like some fabulous monster devouring the darkness in its path.

And then it was gone, and the smell of soot and steam drifted down to me upon the cold air.

I turned back towards the boy. But, once again, he had slipped away, melting into the darkness, and I was left to try and get my bearings and make my way back alone, only vowing, in my irritation, that when I caught up with him, I would tan his hide for teasing me.

In the end, after half an hour or more of wandering, I stopped a wagon that was going east in the direction of the river, and rode with it, and then got directions which, after one or two false twists and turns, I more or less followed, until I came to the docks, and the streets leading to the inn. Now, I was cold and tired again, I had been far further than was sensible, and for the last mile, walked with a heavy tread indeed. I saw no one now, and the moon had gone behind a fresh bank of cloud. It was the very dead of night. I forgot the boy, poor-looking wretch, lost all interest in anything save my own weariness, and as I flagged, and grew ever tireder, I realised how strange it was that I should long for the sight of that drear, dark, unfriendly inn as if it were home. The smell off the river, when it came to me at last, and the sight of the dim alley that I knew led up to the street, lightened my heart. Yet why should that be so? For where was 'home'? I had no home. If by home I meant a living hearth, a place dear to me, in which there would be a welcome from those to whom I mattered. I had none of these. But, as I went at last down the steps that led off the street to the closed door of the Inn, I resolved that one day I should have those things, and that they would be here in England – though not, perhaps, in the city of London. For I was as sure as anything, after my night's walk, that it was in England that I truly belonged and, moreover, that I had always, from my very beginning, done so.

There was one further incident that night.

The Inn was in darkness. I barred the front door, shot the iron bolts and then felt my way across the hall, groping with my hand outstretched for the stair rail, for there was no window through which the moonlight could penetrate, and no lamp or torch had been left out for me. I thought that by now I knew my way to the upper floors and my own room but at the second landing must have taken a wrong turning, for up here was a warren of short, narrow passageways leading out of one another, and, finding only a blank wall immediately ahead of me, I backed a few yards, before moving cautiously on again. I edged forwards step by step putting my hand out again to keep in contact with the wall on my left. I was afraid of pressing the latch of the wrong door and entering a strange room, uncertain whether to call out, though quite sure that the morose landlord would not thank me for disturbing him.

Then, at the end of the passage, I made out a dim, reddish glow, as if from the last embers of a fire, and began to move towards it, thinking that I might somehow get my bearings there, or at least recognise some familiar-looking corner.

The light did not increase greatly as I drew nearer but seemed to be oddly veiled or obscured. The distance along the corridor was only a few yards, and yet to traverse it took an eternity, I was so tired and dazed.

Then, abruptly, I came much closer to the source of the light, and at the same moment, missed my footing on the single step that was in my way. I reached out my arm, flailing, to save myself and just managed to do so, but I reeled nonetheless, and my hand touched not empty air, nor any solid wall or door but instead, to my horror, came up against and went straight through a screen or curtain made of beads that clung and trailed about me like skeins as I stumbled, so that I felt them not only on my hands and arms but about my head and face too. The sensation in the darkness was a horrible one, but worse was to follow.

Looking up I saw that the curtain did indeed cover an open doorway and that behind a small, dark inner lobby, at the entrance to which I was now standing, lay a room. I could make out little and my impression of it was swift and muddled, in my own confusion and the shock of almost falling. I saw a round table and, beside it though set back a little, a chair, in which sat an old woman. The glow came from a single dim lamp which stood on the table, its lights veiled by some kind of reddish-coloured cloth. The woman wore a scarf, tied gypsy-fashion about her forehead, and she seemed to be dressed in shawls of some dark flowing stuff. All of this I no more than glimpsed before she looked up and directly at me, though how much she could see of me in the dimness I do not know. But I saw her. I saw the black pits of her eyes with a pin-prick gleam at their centre, and a swarthiness and greasiness about her skin; I saw her hands laid on top of one another, old, scrawny, claw-like hands they seemed to me; and the flash of a spark from some jewelled or enamelled ring.

It has taken minutes to describe, and I break out in a sweat as I re-live the scene, and yet to see the picture of her there beyond the bead curtain in that dark, redly glowing room, took only seconds, but in those seconds it impressed itself upon my inner eye and my imagination and memory forever, and awoke some deep, fearful response within me.

I do not know whether I cried out, I only know that I recoiled almost at the very instant of first feeling the curtain and seeing the old woman, and backed away, stumbling again, wrenching my hands from the wretched, clinging strands – I can still hear the soft slack noise of its falling off me and back upon itself as I fled. But in my haste I fell again, this time against a piece of furniture set back to the wall, and jarred myself badly and, through the noise and my own cursings, heard a peremptory voice and saw a light, as a door at the end of the passage was opened.

The landlord showed me the way back to my room, from which I had been only a few paces, with an ill grace, and I could not have blamed him for that, but in fact I was very little aware of his sullen complaints and remonstrations, I was so caught up within my own disorientation and fear.

I did not come to or calm myself until I had been alone for some time, sitting in the silence on my bed. I had been badly frightened, not by the dark nor by losing my way of course, those were trivial matters, but by what I had seen, the old crone draped in her gypsy-like scarves and shawls, sitting at a table in a dark room before a veiled lamp. Yet rack my brains as I might I could think of nothing in the reality of that to terrify a grown man who had travelled alone to some of the remotest parts of the world and seen almost daily sights a thousand times more horrifying and strange. My heart had pounded and was still beating too fast, my mouth was dry, my brain seemed to burn and crackle with the over-alertness of a state of nervous dread. Yet why? I had to conclude that I was not frightened by what I had actually seen so much as by some memory it had stirred, or something that had terrified me long ago. I could recall nothing, though I beat at my brains for most of that night, for I did not sleep again until dawn. I only knew that, whenever I saw the old woman with my inner eye, I started back, wanting desperately to get away, avoid the sight of her face and figure, her look, and, above all, to avoid entering the darkened room that lay beyond the beaded curtain.

CHAPTER THREE

I spent the following week walking about London, and with every day that passed the dreadful nightmare glimpse of the old woman receded from my mind and my nerves became quite steady again, for nothing else at all disturbing or untoward came about, and it was a week of remarkably fine weather, with clear cold air and brightness in the sky both early and late.

In that week I came to know the great city as well as any man who does not live in it for years; I gave myself over to it. I walked the length of the River Thames, and up to the Hampstead heights, I walked south and east far along the wide roads leading out to the country, I paced around square after square of graceful, fashionable houses, and lost myself repeatedly in the maze of huddled, smoky terraces that cluster behind the railway stations of Euston and St Pancras, Marylebone and Victoria. I went among the lawyers in their shady courts and ancient inns, I stood deafened by the thundering of all the presses of Fleet Street and strolled with the throngs up Ludgate Hill and through the Park and down Piccadilly. I looked at towers and palaces and statues and monuments, I came to recognise the cries of costers and flower girls, paper-sellers and draymen.

I walked in the half-empty streets among the milk carts and hurrying clerks at early morning, and again and again took to them at night, in every well-lit thoroughfare and dim side-alley. I drank my fill of London and was intoxicated by it.

Some weeks before embarking on my voyage to England I had written two letters, the first to an antiquarian bookseller and private publisher of a few monographs of biography and travel who, I had reason to know, had some interest in the voyages of Conrad Vane, and the second to the High Master of the public school Vane had attended, some twenty miles up the river from London.

On the Friday of that week I went to the shipping company offices to make arrangements for the continued storage of my bags, for I had not yet decided in which part of London I wished eventually to take rooms, and there found replies from both men suggesting that I make contact with them when I arrived in England.

I now did so, and arranged to meet the Reverend Archibald Votable, High Master of Alton, at the Athenaeum Club in Pall Mall, but first, to visit Mr Theodore Beamish's bookshop and offices in the district of Holborn.

I found the shop with much difficulty. It stood in the middle of a row of tall, narrow brick houses that formed the east side of Crab Passage, a dark cobbled thoroughfare in the vicinity of Chancery Lane. It seemed to be unnamed on any map and unheard of by the passers-by from whom I sought directions, and I finally came upon it by accident, after cutting in and out, and had almost left it by the other side, for it was very short and bore no sign, when I caught sight of books, stacked from floor to ceiling, through the window of what I at first took to be a private dwelling, set between a dingy pipe and tobacco shop and a pair of high wooden gates leading to a drayman's yard. It was only when I turned back and went to examine the place more closely that I saw the worn lettering Theo. Beamish, Book-seller, on a plate beside the door.

Although it was another afternoon of winter sunlight out in the open streets, here in the passage, and especially within the shop, no brightness penetrated, and the blue sky was visible only in fragments, like chips of mosaic, above the buildings.

Three stone steps led up to the door of the shop, which led directly into the ground floor room that ran some distance back. There was scarcely space to edge sideways between the shelves and stacks of books, mainly volumes of biography, history and travel, with many relating to the east. I hovered for some moments, getting my bearings and adjusting my eyes to the dimness – there was no light other than what filtered through the tall window, but no one emerged, so that at last I climbed a short steep staircase that led to an upper room, also full of books, but here the shutters were half-closed, so that I could not make any attempt to examine them. Next to this room was a cubby hole of an office containing a huge, overflowing desk, and stacks of boxes and piles of paper.

A doorbell had jangled rather rustily as I entered the shop below, my footsteps had echoed on the bare wooden floorboards as well as on my mounting the stairs but still no one came out to greet me, or enquire my business, no one seemed aware of or interested in my presence in the place at all.

I looked along the shelves at random, picking up a volume here and there, until I came upon a book about that part of China in which I had travelled only a few years previously, along the route set by Conrad Vane, and where I found most evidence of his presence. I opened it eagerly but as I began to turn the pages, I became aware of a strange, uncomfortable sensation. At first, it felt as if I were being watched and the impression was so strong that twice I looked sharply from the pages and over my shoulder around the room, and finally towards the window. But there was no one, I was quite alone, and there was no sound save for the crisp turning of the pages under my hand. But the sensation did not leave me, and mingled with it was a prickle of unease, as though some sixth sense were warning me of danger. But what possible danger could there be? The sense of being observed became insistent, willing me to take notice of it, but again, on glancing round, even moving about the room and looking in every direction, I saw no one.

The shop was very cold, and the air musty with the smell of old books, but now I smelled something else, a very faint, distinctive and strangely sweet odour. It was pungent and yet the trace was so slight that, when I inhaled more deeply in an effort to identify it, it was lost. But I knew it, and it was linked to some place, some situation I had been in. For a few seconds there was a swirl in my brain as I struggled to place it, snatches of confused images, sounds, colours, together with an odd sensation of instability or faintness, yet it was all so fleeting I could scarcely grasp anything of it before it was gone, and the smell was gone too, as if it had never been. I concluded that, as I had turned a page or two of the book, some dust of an old fragrance, perhaps a perfume, a spice, a pressed flower petal, that had been lingering there had been released, and a last vestige of it had entered my nostrils, before it had disintegrated into the surrounding air.

I set the book carefully on the shelf, and as I did so, turned my head quickly. In the street outside stood the boy. He was dressed in the same, ragged, collarless shirt as before, but this time he looked even frailer, and distressed rather than merely preoccupied or distant, his mouth pinched, his eyes huge and hollow, and bright, as if he had a fever. But it was his expression which struck me with such force, and awoke an immediate response from deep within me, and chilled and frightened me too, it was one of such fear and misery and desperation, a pleading, anguished look that he directed at me, so that I could do no other than plunge out of the shop to try and reach him, rescue him – I scarcely knew what. But, as I flung open the door and hurtled down the steps into the lane, I was almost put on my back by a huge, gangling youth coming up to the shop door, and colliding with me. In his arms was a broad shallow basket, covered in a cloth, from which a hot savoury smell arose, and as I reeled backwards and tried to recover myself, he said reproachfully, 'Mr Monmouth I take it, sir, and this 'n's your and Mr Beamish's dinner you had nearly spread across the street.'

In dusting myself off and apologising and making way for him and his tray, in my embarrassment and confusion, I had barely a second in which to glance around Crab Passage. The boy was gone.

So the feeling that I was being watched had been real enough, and perhaps followed too, all over London, else how could he have possibly come across me in this obscure, unmarked alley?

Had the young man with his tray not been standing waiting for me at the top of the shop steps I would have made some attempt to track down the boy's hiding place, for apart from being bewildered at his abrupt, silent appearances, I was now concerned about his welfare, so ill and ragged did he look.

But I could do no more now. I turned and went behind the youth into the shop and straight up the stairs, past the first floor office and then on up a further rickety flight, holding firmly to the banister, for it was pitch dark. At the top stood a closed door, which we went through into a small lobby, and up to a second door, against which the youth bumped his shoulder.

'Come.'

I thought the voice was that of a woman, it was so high-pitched.

[33]

'Shove,' the boy said, and held the door open for me to follow. I realised that he was announcing his own name.

I stepped cautiously forward.

It was an extraordinary room, running, so far as I could make out, the full length of the top of the house, with windows overlooking the rooftops. It was gloomy, the walls were lined with leather-bound books, there were heavy curtains of dark green plush fabric with deep pelmets, and the table and armchairs were draped in it too. An ornate black marble fireplace filled the wall at the far end, over which hung a huge, carved, gilded mirror, and as I glanced into it, I caught the first glimpse of my host, reflected in it. I turned round.

He was seated in a low chair near to the window, his arms, with their podgy little hands, folded over an immense, rotund belly. He had small, piercing eyes, a bald, domed head, and he was very formally dressed, like a lawyer, in an old-fashioned suit with gold watch and chain across the waistcoat.

'Mr Beamish?'

'I am, sir.'

A man, yes, but with the high, squeaking voice I had mistaken for that of a woman or even a child.

He did not rise, but gestured to the seat opposite.

'Shove will be gone presently,' he said.

'I had not realised that you were offering me dinner. I am most grateful.'

'Snecker's pies.'

'Mutton,' Shove said over his shoulder.

He had laid the table, and was now setting out tankards and a jug of ale.

'I came into the shop some time ago – I even ventured upstairs, but no one was about and no one seemed to hear me.'

'I heard you.' His small eyes were upon me. They were

cold and his expression complacent, and I saw that he got pleasure from trying to discomfort me. I did not take to him.

'People come and go. Shove's about the place. They generally know what they want.'

'You've a remarkable stock. I found much to interest me.'

'I take it you've travelled, Mr Monmouth?'

'Indeed.'

'I have not. I let others travel for me.' He gestured to the books.

'Right,' Shove said.

Mr Beamish began to heave himself to his feet and totter over to the dining table – I thought that it might be as far as he ever went. As well as being fat he was short, no more than five feet or so, so that as he moved he seemed to rock backwards and forwards like a child's toy. Everything about him should have made for cheeriness and jollity of personality but it did not. Sitting down with him at the table, I felt that I wanted to keep him at arm's length and that there was no warmth or humour, other than of a sarcastic kind, in him. Nevertheless he was hospitable to a stranger, I was hungry, and curious about him and his business, and above all anxious that he should give me as much information as possible on the subject of Conrad Vane.

With the hot mutton pies there were peas, mashed potatoes and gravy and the ale to drink, and Mr Beamish did not speak at all while he ate, but tucked a white napkin under his chin and attacked his food with complete, and vigorous, concentration.

I took the opportunity during the pauses between mouthfuls to glance about me – indeed, I was able to peer, for Mr Beamish was busy concentrating on his food. As well as the books and the heavy furniture and curtains I noticed several peculiar objects, all of them singularly unpleasant. On the sideboard stood a glass dome beneath which was not the usual arrangement of dried flowers or waxen fruit but a curious tree stump or piece of old driftwood of a most twisted and tortured shape, out of which at various points sprouted weird fungoid growths intertwined with one another, the colour of old bone or parchment. There was a shield made of stretched, stained skin, and a tiny shrunken head on a stand, clumps of spongy, lava-like rock and several objects I could not identify, floating in sealed jars of murky liquid.

At the far end of the room stood a handsome pair of globes and, beside them, a map display case.

Mr Beamish sucked down the dregs of his ale, and wiped his little pursed, pink mouth.

'What set you onto Vane?' He was looking at me closely.

I said, 'Many years ago I came upon a book in my Guardian's collection – we were living in Africa then. I began it for want of anything else to read at the time and could not leave off – it opened up the world to me, places, voyages, and it made mention of various travellers. One of them was Conrad Vane.'

'What do you know of him?'

'That he first journeyed across . . .'

'No, no, not where, *him*.'

Beamish had arrived at once at the nub of my reason for being here.

'Precious little,' I said at last, 'I am hoping that you, among others, can tell me much more.'

'You will find little.'

'Just the same . . .'

'Why?'

I blustered. He was making me feel uncommonly nervous and unsure of myself.

'I suppose – well, it is simply a task that I have set myself. It attracts me. And I have nothing else to do.'

[36]

'Then you should make it your business to find something,' he said softly. I stared.

'Leave be, Mr James Monmouth. That is my advice to you. Leave be.'

'Why on earth . . .'

'Reasons.'

'Good heavens, man, you are trying to make a dark mystery out of all this.'

'Not I.'

'I have already followed in Vane's footsteps across half the world.'

'And came alive out of it.'

'Certainly. Oh, I have been in peril enough but that is the risk the adventurous traveller takes.'

'Do you know of Catchment? Dawes? Luis van Ray?'

'A little . . . not of the last. They were names I heard mentioned in the course of my travels, they had been ahead of me.'

'And where are they now?'

'I do not . . .'

'Dead, Mr James Monmouth. Dead – or vanished.'

'As I said, it is a perilous business.'

'Not in the usual way. They did not die or disappear because they fell among thieves or down a ravine.'

'I do not understand you.'

'Leave be.'

'Mr Beamish . . .'

'You've travelled. You are safely returned. Your luck held. Don't tempt fate.'

'Fate? How? Here in England, in the safety of this snug little island? Here, where I intend to settle, to find a place to live, here where I shall do no more than read and write and diligently pursue my own researches, and where my only adventures will be among gentle hills and downs, and over moorland to the sea? Where I shall travel by rail and on foot? Where I shall talk to those who can inform me and otherwise think my own thoughts? Here where I shall be like an old horse put out to grass?' I almost laughed in his face.

'Here,' he said, 'here will be the most perilous of all.'

The man, I decided, was mad and the look on my face must have told him that I thought so.

'No one,' he said, 'wants to revive the memory or disturb the shade of Conrad Vane. No one will speak to you of him – no one who could possibly be of any use to you. No one who knows.'

'Knows what?'

'What he knows.'

'This is gibberish.' I stood. I was angry now. But I thought that I had seen through him. Theodore Beamish wanted to put me off, to frighten me in some way so that I would leave the study of Conrad Vane, his life and work, to someone else – himself.

'I do not know what nonsense you are trying to fill me with.'

'Sit down, Mr Monmouth . . .'

I would not have done so but at that moment there was a peremptory knock on the door and the youth Shove entered, carrying two covered bowls on his tray.

'Treacle,' he said, set them down on the cloth and lifted the lids. Pudding and custard sat, steaming and fragrant.

For some moments again we ate in silence save for the scraping of spoons. But I was on edge and still annoyed, particularly at the man's attempt to unnerve me. I was also puzzled and above all determined. My plan was to research into the life, especially the early years, of Conrad Vane, for I could not write of his explorations without doing so, and I saw no reason why I should be deterred from carrying it out. Besides, for some reason, the man drew me to him.

Eventually, Mr Beamish set down his spoon and leaned back in his chair.

'Unpleasantness,' he said, 'is to put it mildly.

Unpleasantness. That is what dogs the memory. Did nothing ever strike you? Did no one talk?'

I began to think back to the places I had visited over the past years connected directly with Vane, villages, townships, ancient sites, to the mention I had very occasionally made of him. No, no unpleasantness, as Beamish had it. The most there had been was a kind of blankness, a vague impression gained that Conrad Vane had not been a man remembered, where he was remembered at all, with any particular affection, or whom it was thought right to honour.

'No,' I said at last. 'Nothing.'

'Yet the leopard does not change its spots.'

'You hint at some dark deeds perhaps? Did Vane commit any crime?'

For a second, his eyes narrowed and he shifted his fat little body in the chair. I thought that he was going to tell me something, make a revelation, but he did not; he merely said again, 'Leave be.'

I smiled. 'I have made my first arrangements. I plan to visit Vane's old school. I gather there are some papers, letters and so forth and all his travel writings in manuscript in the library. I intend to take my time in consulting them.'

'You are not a stupid man, Mr Monmouth, not an impulsive young hothead. Why behave as one?'

'That is to insult a guest. You have been hospitable, Mr Beamish, but . . .'

'But you intend to go to hell in your own fashion.'

'Oh come, man!'

'It is evil of which I speak, Monmouth, wickedness, things best left concealed, undisturbed. Whoever is touched by Vane suffers.'

'Mr Beamish, the man is dead.'

'Ah yes.'

'Then of what do we speak?'

'You may ask, you may ask.'

For a split second then, looking into his face, hearing his soft, silken voice in that gloomy room, I was gripped by a cold, dreadful fear. It entered like a splinter of ice going to my heart and I now know that it never truly left me and will not, for the rest of my days. I know that, however vague and odd the tales Beamish was concealing from me, there was some dark truth underlying them, some story of human depravity and misery. Whether he had anything to do with them, whether he had in fact known, or at least met Vane, I could not tell.

Perhaps I could have heeded his words then and put Conrad Vane behind me, and I am sure that it was not mere cussedness and strong will that influenced me. I was not, as Beamish had correctly remarked, a hot-headed young man, I was calm, thoughtful, sober and middle-aged and I wanted a settled and reasonably quiet life. Yet the more he had spoken of Vane, the more fascinated I had become.

But the flash of intense fear I had felt was fleeting and, when it left me, I looked down at the pots on the table, felt my stomach lined and full with warm, comforting food, pie and potatoes, pudding and ale, and the real, straight-forward, everydayness of those things banished into dreamland any hints of other, more shadowy and sinister matters.

The thought of Snecker's mutton pies and ale caused me to dismiss Mr Beamish's warnings and, indeed, to laugh at them.

I thanked him for the dinner, bade him good-day and left. Once again, Shove was nowhere to be seen and the shop was dark and deserted.

I went out quickly and down the steps onto the cobbles, now slippery with rain, of Crab Passage.

CHAPTER FOUR

But I could not shake off Mr Beamish. The picture of him, hands folded complacently over his belly, and the gleam in his small eyes, remained with me all that day and at night he appeared in my uneasy dreams, smiling faintly. I lay awake in the dark early hours, too aware of his closeness.

It was some while before I remembered that I had not seen the boy again.

But Beamish's warnings did not go home, I dismissed them irritably, though from time to time I rehearsed the phrase 'leave be' and wondered what lay behind it.

I was never a stubborn man, young or old, but I was a firm and determined one. All my life, so far as I could remember, I had done what I had set out to do, made my own plans and followed them through and been answerable to no one. Besides, as I had hinted to Beamish, what else was there for me? I was, I confess, still out of place in London and isolated too, without a home, family or friends. I was used to that and did not feel unduly troubled or unhappy, but I needed a purpose, and exploration into the life of Vane was giving me one, for the time being. If I abandoned that, I was uneasily aware that all round me lay vacancy, a pointless, unfocused existence into which I might fall as into a pit. Until now, I had always had an aim, if only a simple one – the next place to make for. I was afraid to lose it and, in losing it, lose also the assurance of my own identity.

None of which I thought through as logically and clearly as I have now set it forth; I only glanced against it and cast a frightened look over my shoulder, as it were, before veering away.

I was beginning to feel less at ease in the Cross Keys Inn, too, and had certainly never felt very welcome there; it was a temporary resting place and, besides, too far out to be convenient. At night, if I did not go walking, because I was tired or the weather was poor, I lay on my bed reading or sat alone and entirely unregarded in the tap room below. In other inns and chop houses about London I struck up conversations, made occasional acquaintances with whom to pass the time of day. Here, I did not. It was an unfriendly place, the customers surly and suspicious, closed in upon themselves and preoccupied with their own affairs. It had served its purpose well enough but I should leave without sentiment or a backward glance. And, although I had never caught sight of the woman in the room beyond the bead curtain again, the thought that I might do so left me apprehensive.

I planned to look for lodgings, either in the city, perhaps in the vicinity of the Law Courts, or else in the congenial neighbourhood of Chelsea, for I had acquired a great affection for London's river, and it would please me to live beside it and become familiar with it in all its phases and aspects.

But, first, I had to keep a second appointment.

I had been in London for almost three weeks, and growing used to it. I daresay that I thought myself by now an urbane and civilised gentleman, but in truth I was a stranger and a foreigner still, in all but a surface veneer of new experience, a man who, for all of his adult life, had travelled in wild, remote and primitive places and lived in cities that bore little relation to this one, whose manners, customs and peoples were different indeed.

I fancied that I had become indistinguishable from any other English gentleman, for so I imagined myself to be, when everything about me, I now realise, must have proclaimed my strangeness.

Once or twice, in the east and in India, I had visited a gentlemen's club, and sat in bamboo chairs under a fan, or else out on a verandah, and drunk whisky and talked with Englishmen, tea planters, civil servants, army men, government officers, so that I assumed that I would feel at home as well in the Athenaeum Club, Pall Mall, as anywhere.

But standing before its great stone pillars, gazing up a flight of steps that led to the entrance door, on that cold December morning, I felt desperately uncertain of myself, and by the time I had summoned up my courage to walk up to that door, my confidence and ease, my blithe assumption of the manner of a London gentleman, had quite evaporated.

At the sight of the vast marble hall and rising staircase, and the glimpses through open doors to formal, panelled rooms beyond, such rooms as I had until now only read of in stories, I all but turned tail and fled. But before I had time to do so, or to gather my wits, I heard a strong Scots voice behind me.

'Mr James Monmouth, I am sure.'

I spun round.

The Reverend Archibald Votable was a man well over six feet tall, broad-shouldered and slightly stooping, handsome, in a florid way, with a jutting brow and dressed in clerical collar and black suit.

His appearance sorted well with the surroundings but his manner was direct and affable, though he looked at me keenly, both as we shook hands and when we were sitting over glasses of madeira before a somewhat reluctant and smoky fire.

I began to feel a little more assured, and at ease with him, too; he was a man who invited confidence.

'As I said in my letter to you some months ago, I understand that the school has papers, manuscripts, letters even, bequeathed in some way from the estate of Conrad Vane. He was a pupil, I know.'

'He was.'

'It would be of great help to me and great interest, if I might consult them.'

He sat, fingertips together. There was no one else in the room, and it was hushed, there were no voices or footsteps, only, at odd moments, the hiss and spurt of the fire.

'I would be glad to hear more about you first, Mr Monmouth.'

Readily, easily, I began to speak, going back to those early days with my Guardian in Africa, re-living my young manhood and then re-visiting, one after another as I spoke, those countries in which I had travelled. My glass was refilled but I only sipped at the sweet wine, I was heady enough with memory and the excitement of recounting my story.

He listened without interruption, eyes for the most part steady on my face, and when at last I had finished, with my arrival in England on that wet night only a few weeks before, he did not speak for some time but looked away from me towards the fire to which a shambling, ancient servant in a baize apron now came, somewhat ineffectually, to attend.

When he had gone and the room had settled back into its church-like hush once more, Mr Votable said, 'I must make it clear at once that there is no bar to your visiting the school and looking up whatever material there may be relating to your subject.'

I thanked him.

'I did not wish merely to hand your letter over, and put the business out of my hands from the beginning. I wanted to meet you, Mr Monmouth, to hear what you had to say, discover what manner of man you are. You seem to me to be an honest one.'

For a moment, he had slipped into a schoolmaster's tone.

'What reason do you have for wanting to research into the life of – this man?' I noted that he did not speak the name.

'I have no more to add to my letter,' I said. 'I have followed in his footsteps for some years, I have read his own accounts of his extraordinary, pioneering travels and explorations. I became interested – for no clear reason that I can give you. But Vane exerts a peculiar fascination upon me – I suppose it has become an obsession, and something to fill what has been a life rather empty of people. Vane became a hero to me.'

'You might find a better.'

'I now gather from other sources that there are rumours of some . . . unpleasantness attaching to his life. A scandal?'

'I think not in any usual sense.'

'I have therefore become all the more intrigued.'

He said quietly, 'Then I have no doubt that you will proceed, no matter what I may advise, and in spite of any admonitions. That is the way of human nature.'

'But I am not reckless or stubborn, Mr Votable, and I would be glad to be told more. I would be grateful for your advice.'

'Then I will give it. Be wary. Such stories – rumours maybe, as I have heard – relate to a time long ago. I had no connection with this man. I only know . . .' He fell silent.

'Sir?'

'No. It is nothing. I will not frighten you with dead men's tales.'

'I am not easily made afraid.'

[45]

'Be wary.'

'But of what? Pray at least be clearer with me. Wary? Of some dreadful danger? What risk am I taking?'

'No, no, no.' He made to sound jovial, dismissive of my fears. 'There is nothing . . . so definite, it will all be coincidence and idle talk.'

'Then why make mention of it at all? Why warn me?'

He stood up. 'Because you are honest, Mr Monmouth. Honest . . . and innocent.'

I left him on the steps of the building, an august, commanding figure. I imagined how a small, recalcitrant boy might feel, sent to stand quaking before him. He had given me an introduction to the school archivist and told me to make arrangements directly with him, once the term was over. There was a set of guest rooms, he said, which I would be welcome to make use of. I got the impression that he was wanting in some measure to retract his words of caution and the hints he had given of something untoward relating to Vane and his life. But it was curious that both he and Mr Beamish – and I trusted the purity of the Reverend Mr Votable's motives more than those of the sinister little bookseller – had tried to warn me away from anything to do with him.

I had not travelled in countries where magic and superstition, legend and myth were powerful without learning to respect the human reaction to those things. Nevertheless, I fancied myself a sober, rational, level-headed man, able to separate reality from fancy, as well as anyone else of vaguely scientific bent.

I had liked Votable, I was grateful to him for his invitation and, for all it had been veiled in oblique warnings, I fully intended to take it up.

CHAPTER FIVE

The Athenaeum Club

Pall Mall

Dear Monmouth,

Further to our meeting and conversation. The school archivist is Dr V. V. Dancer. I have spoken to him and he will make available to you such material as is in our possession. If you would care to contact him he will make all necessary arrangements with regard to your visit.

On another matter, I recall your saying that you seek rooms in proximity to the river. By chance I have heard of some which may be suitable. They are at Number 7, Prickett's Green, Chelsea, S.W. which houses are part of estates belonging to the School.

I have given much thought to the venture you wish to undertake and gone over most carefully in my mind such things as have been mentioned or hinted to me. They are not pleasant things, the man's reputation was a dark one and in certain places unhappy memories linger. But if, as I suppose, you will not be deterred, then again I would urge you, be vigilant, be wary.

I shall not be available for several weeks from today, and would wish you to understand that I prefer to have no further interest in this matter.

Yours etc.

Archibald Votable.

I sat in silence beside the window of my room, the letter open before me on the table. In the dank inn yard below, I could hear the sound of water clattering into a bucket, and a curt order given by the landlord.

The Headmaster had not struck me as a weak man or one who would be easily unnerved but his letter betrayed his fears. He did not wish to have anything more to do with me and my enterprise, because he had spoken to someone about Vane, learned more, perhaps, than he had previously known, and what he had learned had made him afraid.

I was not deterred, but the warning made me pause, and for the first time consider the whole matter rather more seriously. Yet still I knew tantalisingly little. What was supposed to be the danger? What was I being warned against? What was the nature of the stories, rumours, hints, about Conrad Vane, a man some twenty years dead? I felt as if I were groping ahead through a fog, hearing odd whistles and low cries to me to look out, pay heed, but having no clue as to what I was to beware of or in which direction it might lie.

A dog yelped in the yard, yelped again and then fell abruptly silent.

And then, into my mind came a picture of my late Guardian, the man who had raised me from boyhood and helped to direct and mould my character. What would he have done? What advice would he give me now? I knew at once, and also knew without doubt that I would follow it. I would continue with my plans with caution, not dismissing

[48]

the warnings I had been given, however vague, with any false bravado. My Guardian had been a courageous man and an adventurous one. He had also been prudent. I could do no better than try to emulate him.

In the meantime, I intended to call at Number 7, Prickett's Green, S.W.

I found a row of three-storey, stuccoed houses set back behind their own rectangle of garden, with elm trees to either side, overlooking the wide embankment and the River Thames. It was a fine late afternoon, clear and already frosty, the sun low to the west and staining the sky deep crimson and sending gilded darts shooting across the black surface of the water.

I had walked the whole way, keeping the river on my left and revelling in the complementary beauties of sky and river, bare trees and handsome buildings.

Further east the road was busy with traffic, but as I came up to Chelsea it grew quieter. Many times I stopped to lean against the embankment wall and look up and down river, enthralled by all I saw upon it, and then turned to stare at the houses, to admire the elegant proportions, the pleasing roof lines. London, I thought to myself, aware of how deeply I was growing to love it. London.

Above my head, the sky was translucent as enamel. I was a contented man that afternoon.

Number 7, Prickett's Green was at the end of the small row, looking west. Next to it, on the other side of the elm trees, the houses of Cheyne Walk continued.

There was something a little out of sorts about the house. The paint was beginning to peel, the windowpanes were filmed over and altogether the row had been neglected by contrast with its fashionable neighbours, but the shabbiness was oddly reassuring to me and I was in no sense deterred from exploring further. I stood with my back to the river on the far side of the road. The houses were in shadow now, the windows black, vacant eyes, whereas in others, lights shone out from lamps and chandeliers, curtains were draped elegantly back, and thinking of the people in those rooms and of the warm fires, conviviality and comfort, I felt a wave of loneliness and bleakness of spirit rise and break over me, so that I shuddered and hunched down more deeply into the collar of my overcoat. It lasted only a few seconds but it disturbed my serenity of mood and left me uneasy again, and, above all, longing for a companion.

I hurried across the road, and unlatched the low iron gate that let me into the gardens of Prickett's Green.

A note had come from the bursar of the school, giving me directions to the house, and the name of Mr Silas Threadgold, the caretaker, who would admit me. But, for some time after I had twice pulled the bell and it had jangled thinly in some distant passage, there was complete silence, and as the house was in darkness and had that indefinably melancholy air suggestive of emptiness, I was about to turn away, thinking, perhaps, of investigating a back entrance, but pulled the bell once more and was answered at last by an irritable voice calling out to me to have patience and heard footsteps dragging along a stone floor.

It was impossible to guess the exact age of Mr Silas Threadgold, who might have been anywhere between fifty and ninety. He was thin, gnarled and twisted in upon himself like an ancient tree, with a bent back, dirty linen and a greasy coat. He opened the front door to me and stood back without a word, so that after a pause I was obliged to take the gesture as an invitation and stepped inside the hall. It was unlit but he turned, still without speaking, and limped ahead of me, and at the foot of the old staircase turned up the gas, which gave some dim illumination to our ascent.

On the first landing, through a narrow window, I looked

out at the sky burning down in the last of its glory, 'red as any blood'.

The boards were bare and sounded loudly to our tread. All the doors we passed were closed.

'I take it the house is empty,' I said, pausing to get my breath.

'Always excepting the basement.'

'In which you live?'

He nodded but did not otherwise reply, and then unlocked a door and, grunting slightly, stood back to let me pass through. As I did so I was unable to restrain my exclamation of surprise and pleasure.

The room extended the whole length of the house, some thirty feet or so, and with three sets of tall windows. I stepped over to them. Below lay the river, almost completely dark now, but still just flushed over its surface by the last light from the sky. And as I looked the lamps began to come on one by one along the embankment and their light formed pools of gold on the river below and made oases on the pathway.

I was on a level with the tree tops that stood to my left and through the black branches I saw the bridge, strung out to the opposite bank, across the water. It was to me as glorious an outlook as I had ever dreamed of, the rooms were perfect for this reason alone and I knew that I would take them no matter what – though they were more than adequately furnished, if shabby, and I could buy any small extra comforts at will. Apart from the main sitting room there were three other, utilitarian rooms, including a small dressing room that also overlooked the river and in which I resolved that I would sleep.

Threadgold had disappeared, clumping off down the stairs without a word to me. I heard a door bang somewhere far below.

I resolved to write to the school, accepting the offer of the rooms, and already planned to move my things out of the

Cross Keys Inn, if possible, the following day, for in spite of the emptiness of the remainder of the house, and the unattractiveness of its caretaker, I knew that I could be settled at last; Number 7, Prickett's Green would be a home to me.

I went back to the window, and saw that the light had now completely faded from the sky.

And then I knew that, when I looked downwards, I should see him, and knew precisely where he would be, huddled close under a lamp. I felt my skin prickle, as though every one of my senses had become more acute. I waited. The house was deathly quiet.

I was not afraid, not on this occasion, though I began to be agitated. More than anything, I felt a sadness and some strange, close affinity with the boy.

Why I had realised the truth at this moment, I did not understand, but I accepted it at once, and was in no doubt, although nothing like it had happened to me in my life, and I knew precious little about such matters.

He stood, pale, ragged, utterly still in the circle of lamp-light and as I stared directly at him he raised his head, turned his face up to me, his eyes seeking mine out. And so we stayed, as if frozen in some other time and place, I, James Monmouth, in the dark, upper room of the house, and the ghost of the boy in the cold street below.

And then I did become afraid, with a strange, very calm fear that so chilled me as almost to stop my blood in its course. I was bewildered too and yet still drawn to him as by an invisible beam of almighty strength. The look he gave me was so full of anguish and misery, of desperation and pleading, and of a sort of blame, too, so that I felt not angry and irritated with him as before but deeply guilty, as though I had known and betrayed him. I knew that there was no earthly point in my leaving the window and the house and running down the path and over to him, for when I reached the lamp he would certainly be gone. I could say nothing, ask nothing. Yet there was something I should surely do for him, his appearances meant as much, I was certain. But what? How? And how might I discover?

Lights from a barge, moving down river, sparkled on the water. I followed it out of sight and then brought my gaze slowly back. But he had stepped out of the bright ring, and was gone.

I bent my head for a second and closed my eyes, and most earnestly and urgently prayed for guidance and protection.

Two days later I had arranged for my trunks to be collected from the shipping company's warehouse and moved out from the Cross Keys Inn – from where I was bade the most cursory of farewells – and into the rooms at Number 7, Prickett's Green. Within a few days I had purchased some extra pieces of furniture and linen, arranged with Silas Threadgold to have breakfast brought up each morning and found a good coffee house half a mile's walk away, where I could eat my evening dinner. The weather continued cold, bright and clear and my spirits remained high.

I did not see the boy again and indeed, with some curious extra sense I seemed to be developing, knew that I would not. All was open, cheerful and unremarkable. I was too busy about my domestic matters to think much at all of Conrad Vane but I planned to settle myself and then to travel down to the school and spend some days there, making a start on my work.

I acquired a desk and chair which I placed in one window and a wing armchair which I drew close up to another and, seated at one or other of them, I spent many hours during those first days simply watching the river, its traffic, the play of the sun and shadow upon the water, the movement of the tides. I paid less attention to the passers-by along the embankment but in them too was a measure of diversion and interest, so that I never tired of the scene.

The rest of the house was, I still supposed, empty – at least I saw no one other than the lugubrious Threadgold. Whether he had a wife, or any other companion, in the basement I did not enquire.

I had slept remarkably well right through every night, waking each morning as the dawn came up, well after seven o'clock, and going at once to look out upon the river and the sky above it and to await the arrival of breakfast, which I ate also at the window.

But on the fifth night I came wide awake abruptly, long before morning, and, being somewhat cold, got up at once, thinking of finding extra covering for my bed.

I had left the curtains undrawn as usual, and the light of the moon shone in, slanting silver across the floor. I went to the window. The lamps were out but the moonlight lay over the water, still and beautiful, and as I watched, some small, dark craft slipped across its path and was illumined by it, before blending back into the shadows again.

Cold as I was I could not bear to return to my bed, but stood for some while looking with deep satisfaction at all I saw. And then I heard a woman singing. The sound seemed to come from somewhere distant, perhaps far below in the house, I could not be sure. It was a soft, low, sad, murmuring voice, a little like that of one crooning a child to sleep, or else keening faintly, absorbed in distress.

I strained to hear it more clearly but could not and at last went to the outer door and opened it. Landing and stairs were in darkness and there was complete silence. There was no one at all below, I was quite sure, I heard not a creak of the boards, not a breath upon the musty air. I thought momentarily of creeping down and stopping to listen at each door, but in the end only returned to my room. There, as I became still, I again heard the woman's voice, and then I was a little afraid, but the voice awakened something else in me, some deep longing, some memory so dim and far back that it was unrecognisable, indecipherable.

I went to look out but there was no one, either on the near or far pavement or on the wide roadway between, and in the gardens nothing moved, either in the still, eerie moonlight or among the shadows.

What was happening to me, why I had seen the boy, and now heard the singing, why I was such easy prey to so many emotions as a result I did not understand, but strangely, as I stood there in the middle of the night, alone in my rooms, I was quite calm and undisturbed, only bewildered, and strangely out of touch with my own self and the feelings and responses I was experiencing.

It was a long time before, shivering, I returned to my bed and slept, and slept well until morning and the noise of the caretaker hammering on the door.

I felt rested and clear of purpose. The incidents of the previous night had not faded from my mind but I was sure that I needed to give myself something to occupy me completely and decided to put down both my repeated sightings of the boy and now the sound of the woman's voice singing, when I was sure no woman had been by, to some sort of nervous strain whose cause I could not fathom but which had better be dealt with by vigorously plunging myself into work. I had been too idle, too self-absorbed, too many hours had been spent ambling purposelessly about, or staring idly out of windows.

Accordingly, after a hurried breakfast, I set out to make my arrangements.

CHAPTER SIX

The fine weather changed on the morning of my departure.
A raw wind blew off the river, finding its way mercilessly
through my inadequate light overcoat and the sky was
thick and curded with low steely clouds. Because of a mis-
calculation in the time of ordering my cab and congestion
in the streets, I arrived at Waterloo with scarcely a minute
to spare and was obliged to run along the platform and
jump into the first available compartment.

The guard's whistle blew as the door slammed shut and I
found myself alone with a striking-looking woman who was
surrounded by suitcases, bags and hat-boxes and sitting
with a very upright posture in the opposite seat. I removed
my hat and muttered an apology for my precipitate entry
but she merely inclined her head very slightly and looked
away. I noted how well she was dressed in a long, fur-
trimmed coat of dark purple wool, with a high fur collar,
muff and hat. Her hands, which were folded in her lap,
were studded with heavy diamond and emerald rings and I
judged her, from my covert glances, to be in the prime of
her middle years, wealthy and well connected.

To my pleasure the train ran for some way alongside the
Thames, before branching off – we were to pick it up again

at the end of our journey. But it was a dismal view, the outskirts of London and then the countryside dull and grey under a gathering sky, and before long I turned away to read my newspaper. When I glanced up again it was because of a change in the light and, looking out, I saw that it had begun to snow. I was not able to suppress an exclamation of pleasure and wonder for, whatever I may have known in childhood, as a grown man I had not seen snow, and sat mesmerised by the swirling flakes and fast-whitening fields as the train ran on. Then the lamps came on in the carriage and at once the outside world seemed to darken and recede, though now and again fat snowflakes splattered silently on the windows before being at once blown off again.

We stopped at a station, and then another, but no one got into our compartment. I went on with my paper, though I was repeatedly drawn from it towards the snow and as I did look up I became conscious that the woman opposite was regarding me steadily. I did not so much see it, for I did not turn my head towards her, or catch her eye, as sense her look upon me, and in the end was made uncomfortable by it and would have spoken, had we not just then stopped at a small station. No one waited on the platform, no one left or boarded the train but we did not move off, only waited in the cold and silence, the luggage rack creaking occasionally above our heads. I looked out. There was not even a porter on the platform. Above the roof, the snow was like feathers flying about the sky.

'Go back.'

I spun round. She had spoken in a low but quite firm, clear tone. 'I beg your pardon?'

Her eyes were very blue, and slightly widened, and they stared not so much at as into me, and yet there was a strange, distant expression in them, as though she were seeing not me but something beyond.

'You should not go. I sense it very strongly. You must stay away.'

Into my head came Beamish's voice, 'Leave be', and Votable's 'Be wary', and I shuddered involuntarily and shrank back in my seat from the woman's stare, feeling suddenly afraid of these apparently random but adamant warnings. I did not believe in gypsy prophecies or other superstitions of that kind but there had been too many odd hints and happenings. I was watching her face. Quite suddenly her expression changed, she came out of her trance-like state. Her eyes focused upon me and she smiled and coloured faintly. 'I must apologise. But when it is so clear I cannot help myself. It comes without warning. From the moment you entered the compartment . . .'

'Madam . . . ?'

'My name is Viola Quincebridge. My husband is Sir Lionel – the judge.'

'I am afraid I am new to England, Lady Quincebridge, I know almost no one, have heard of no one.' I held out my hand to her. 'James Monmouth.'

'Yes, of course. You have been a traveller. You . . .' Her face clouded again. 'But it is not the past – or not altogether . . . it is the future.'

'I must ask what you know of me.'

'Nothing. I have neither seen nor heard of you before today.'

The compartment was absolutely silent, apart from her low, urgent voice. We were still standing at the deserted country station. Now and again there came a faint hiss of steam, or iron clang, from the engine ahead. I saw that the edge of the platform was now white with lying snow.

'It is sometimes very awkward – an embarrassment, that I know – am told, these things – am given warnings. I become so horribly aware of, oh, an imminent death, danger, of evil surrounding someone – usually a person I do not know at all, but very occasionally it is a friend, which is

[58]

the worst. It has happened to me since I was a child. I never try to influence it, bring it about, very much the contrary, but it is so powerful I cannot ignore it.'

I saw that she spoke the truth.

'And have these – feelings ever proved correct?'

'Oh yes, always – when I know the outcome, that is. Of course I very often do not . . .' She pulled her collar closely around her throat. It was becoming bitterly cold in the carriage.

'I do not choose,' she said quietly.

Then, I found myself beginning to speak about myself, and to tell her, though quite guardedly at first, of my years abroad and a little about the recent weeks in London. I finished by outlining, very matter of factly, my plans for the immediate future, and the work on Conrad Vane.

'It is in that connection,' I said, 'that I am travelling today. I am on my way to his old school, where the library has papers, letters and so forth. I intend to stay there for a few days and begin my researches.'

Her face remained clouded and thoughtful. 'And then?'

'Then? Oh, I shall return to my rooms in Chelsea – unless my quest leads me elsewhere, which at this stage I cannot foresee.'

'What will you do at Christmas, Mr Monmouth?'

'I confess I have given it no thought whatsoever.'

It was true. In past years, in those countries I had lived and travelled in, Christmas had meant little or nothing and, although I had been brought up as a Christian and sent to a missionary school, I had grown away from observance of the ceremonies as soon as I had left – though not altogether from some simple, essential beliefs.

'The day will soon pass,' I said, 'without very much interest.'

She opened her handbag and took out a card.

'That is our address. We are only a few miles or so from the school – my sons went there, of course, so did my husband. If you have need of anything at all during your stay . . .'

I took it and thanked her.

'I am so uneasy. I wish you would not go on with this. I do not know why but I feel it so strongly.'

I did not reply.

'Ah, you think I am mad, a hysterical, middle-aged woman. I have embarrassed you, I see that.' She leaned forward and spoke urgently. 'It has been so very long – years, since it has happened to me. I assure you that I am in all respects very calm and common-sensical.'

'I believe it.'

'Come to us for Christmas. Yes, that is the answer! We shall be quite a large party, you will fit in perfectly. I can't think of your being alone in a strange country at Christmas.'

'It is not strange – I have never felt more at home.'

'Nevertheless.'

'You are very kind. But you do not know me – you know nothing about me.'

'I know what you have told me, and it is quite clear to me that you are an honest man.'

I remembered that the Reverend Mr Votable had said as much.

'Thank you. But surely your husband . . .'

'Oh, Lionel will not object, he will find you of great interest, I assure you, and he is always guided by me in such domestic arrangements. Come to us at Christmas, Mr Monmouth. Telegraph to us, giving your arrival time, and I will arrange to have you met at the station – say, on Christmas Eve?'

At that moment, the train jerked and started to move slowly forwards, we cleared the bleak little station and were at once plunged into a blackness through which snow whirled furiously. Lady Quincebridge settled back, took out a pair of spectacles and a book, and I returned to my paper and for the rest of the journey we read in companionable silence. But I felt a warmth and pleasure within me as a result of her invitation. I had made a friend, the first since my arrival in England, and I welcomed it. Her odd warnings and forebodings I preferred to set quietly aside.

When the train slowed again and then pulled into the riverside station at which I was to alight, she extended her hand.

'I continue a little further down the line,' she said, peering at me in a wholly cheerful and friendly manner over the top of her glasses. 'Now I shall expect to hear from you.'

I bade her goodbye and turned to set my bag down on the platform. It was only as I slammed the heavy train door that she called out something else, but over the noise of the engine and the clang of a porter's trolley I could not make it out, I only saw her expression which was again one of alarm and anxiety – the sight of her distraught face was to return often to my mind in the weeks to come.

For the moment, though, I was occupied in finding my way out of the station and taking directions for the school, which I was told lay about a mile ahead. In spite of the weather, I rejected a cab and, carrying my own bag, walked out into the snow-covered street and turned right, to cross the bridge that spanned the river.

Here, the Thames curved slightly towards me, wide and fast-flowing, and I stood and looked over into the water. The snow had almost stopped falling now and there was a crack in the clouds through which a little moonlight shone. The air was cold and a slight breeze blew from downriver. I turned. Ahead of me stretched a long, narrow high street, with the roofs of small houses and shops clustered together on either side, low-lying and sloping at different angles, and all covered with thick, freshly fallen snow. Here and there, lights shone out onto the pavement, but the roadway was white and untrammelled. The air smelled wonderfully of the snow and my spirits were high, I felt excitement, as if something miraculous were about to happen, and a complete absence of any sense of strangeness or apprehension. The dark warnings of Lady Quincebridge on the train now only seemed amusing.

An old man, muffled in heavy scarves and a long, shabby tweed coat, came shambling towards me, and I bade him a cheerful good evening. He nodded, peering at me out of rheumy eyes, but after that the bridge and the street ahead were empty again.

I walked on, treading carefully through the snow, for I had no boots or overshoes, and kept close to the shop fronts and houses, where it lay more thinly. Inside the bakers' and grocers', cobblers' and outfitters' and alehouses, lights glowed warmly behind steamed-up windows, and I saw the shadows of those moving about within, but out here I was entirely alone, making my way towards where I began to see the ancient building of the school, the tower, the chapel, the old walls rising up, dark and imposing. Apart from the gas lamps, all was dark, and silent, save for the soft press and creak of my own footsteps upon the snow. The moon had gone behind the clouds again. I stopped and set down my bag and my breath plumed out like silver smoke in front of my face.

To my right stood a wooden door with a square grille and a brass bell handle set into the wall beside it. I went over, pulled it and listened to the clang and, as I waited then, the snow began to fall lightly again, the huge flakes settling gently like goose-down on my shoulder and sleeve. I found it beautiful beyond all expressing, and the cold and snow and the silent darkness were home to me, familiar, fitting; I remembered and responded to them, and realised that, when I was a child, they must have formed part of the background to my life. There was some secret, just out of reach, the answer to a mystery, and, if I had been able to stand there for long enough, I felt I would have guessed it, been given an answer and understood it. But then there

[62]

was a scraping sound and the metal grille was lifted. Behind it, I saw the outline of a face, and a muffled light.

I spoke my name and heard the bolts being drawn back, and the veil fell forward again, the secret was secret still.

The porter who admitted me was a ruddy-faced man wearing a bowler hat and greatcoat. He took my bag and, after locking and bolting the wooden door again, led me out from under the shadow of the buildings. As we passed by his lodge, I glanced in and saw a cosy, frowsty room, with an armchair pulled up close to a grate in which a small fire was burning, and, beside it, a black cat, curled asleep.

We came out into a great, rectangular cobbled yard, surrounded on four sides by dark buildings, several of which he pointed out as we passed. 'Chapel', and 'Scholars' House', and 'Muniments', though without any explanation, and then stopped before a statue on a plinth in the centre.

'King Henry,' he said curtly.

The King stood, grave and venerable, with snow on his leaden shoulders. Ahead was a clock tower. 'The King's Tower.' I paused and looked back. Snow covered the cobbles and the stone window-ledges, giving off a pale sheen, and a pool of light bobbed ahead from the porter's lantern. Everything else was hidden deep in shadow, and now we passed under an archway into an inner cloister, and here the shadows lay deeper still. A passage ran round the parameters of the snow-covered central square, with arches at regular intervals. We walked around three sides, our footsteps echoing hollow on the stone floor, and the echoes were taken up and continued to sound all around us, so that I had the urge to whisper aloud and hear the answering echo.

It was cold as iron here but, at last, we ascended a flight of stone steps, went through a baize door, and into a wood-panelled corridor. Several closed doors stood on one side,

[63]

and, on the other, windows in stone embrasures looked down into the court. The walls were lined with portraits, whose eyes seemed to follow me, staring down, and I had an uneasy sense that all around us and behind doors, hidden in corners, standing back in the shadows, faces watched, saw us pass, took note. But, when I looked, there was no one.

We stopped in front of a door, and the porter set down my bag. 'Here is your set, sir. Everything you should require. Dr Dancer is away until tomorrow, sir, but I am to conduct you to the library after breakfast, which I will bring. And so, sir, I bid you goodnight.' He leaned forward, through the doorway, and switched on a light. 'At the top of the two flights. There is a bell, sir, connecting to the lodge, should you require anything.'

'Thank you.' I picked up my bag. 'Thank you very much.'

But he was already off down the corridor; the baize door sighed shut and I was left alone in the silence that seethed like dust, settling around me.

A steep flight of stairs led ahead, twisted sharply round and narrowed even more for a second, shorter flight, at the top of which was another baize door. My footsteps trod heavily on bare boards and I was half-expecting to come out into some dingy attic furnished with spartan iron bed-stead in the style of a school dormitory, without comforts of any kind. It was still bitterly cold and a draught came through cracks on every side. I reflected that, since my arrival in England, I had spent much time climbing stairs up to strange rooms, wondering what lay ahead, and I was becoming, after so many odd, unnerving events, more and more wary and apprehensive. I need not have been.

On pushing open the door, I found myself at once in a most pleasing and comfortable sitting room. The lamps were lit, a fire burned brightly in the grate, with a brass hod full of coal beside it and logs neatly stacked on either side.

There was a desk and a fine mahogany table, deep arm-chairs, books in the bookshelves, a good Persian rug, bowls of fruit and nuts on a sideboard – I felt as if the room had been waiting like a friend, for my arrival, and I sat down, still in my overcoat, closed my eyes and, involuntarily, a great sigh of relief and contentment rose up from deep within me, and I shed, as I exhaled, all the anxiety, weari-ness, fear – yes, it had been a form of fear that I had been so bowed down and cramped by all that day and for several days past.

And, as I sat, from across the roof-tops a gentle bell chimed and then sounded the hour, and the sound was a sweet one, lulling me even further into tranquillity.

The rest of the set, when I bestirred myself to explore it, consisted of a small bathroom, and a bedroom more plainly, but nonetheless adequately, furnished and equip-ped, and containing a long carved and gilded mirror, fixed to the wall opposite the window. The sight of it made me start. I had seen the mirror before, it was so familiar that I thought back to my Guardian's bungalow, all those years before, wondering if perhaps one like it had hung there, but I was sure that it had not, there had been nothing so ornate in that sober little house. I stared at the mirror again, puzzled, tracing over every scroll and curlicue, certain that I had done so many times before, searching in the depths of my memory. But I was forced to give up, I had no clue as to where I had previously seen it.

From the sitting room window, as I parted the heavy velvet curtains and looked down, I could just make out snow-covered gardens and playing fields, stretching away into the darkness. But the bedroom overlooked the main school yard, the cobbles, the King's statue and the side of the towering chapel.

The day's newspapers and some journals were set out upon the desk, decanters of sherry and port stood on a table. I unpacked, bathed and, comfortable in robe and slippers, warmed myself with a glass, beside the fire.

I had brought fresh writing books and a set of new pencils and these I set out, fully determined that first thing the next morning, on being conducted to the library, and shown the Vane archive, I would assume the mantle of scholar and biographer, and work quietly and steadily through the next few days. The vision appealed to me greatly, for though I had been a traveller for so long, an adventurer even, and rarely settled in any one place, I had read and studied and tried to make up for the gaps in my education and had even written, too, perhaps in emulation of Vane, some slight descriptive articles about the east and my journeys there. I began to dream now, sitting by the bright fire, of seeing my name in gold letters on the spines of impressive volumes, hearing myself referred to as 'James Monmouth the scholar, Monmouth the writer'.

My harmless fantasies were interrupted briefly by the arrival of a tray of supper, simple, excellent food, cooked, he said, by the porter himself, 'school's being down, sir, and therefore the cook's away'. He also brought a letter from Dr Dancer, come by the late post.

My dear Monmouth,

This is to welcome you to Alton, and to apologise for my unavoidable absence this evening. I trust you will find all comfortable and to your convenience and liking. Biglow will see to things for you, and I shall expect to be with you tomorrow morning – I return very late tonight, weather permitting, but will not disturb you – to give you as much help as I am able, though that, I fear, will be little enough. Would you give me the pleasure of dining with me tomorrow evening?

Yours etc.

Valentine Dancer.

Later, in pulling out my watch to wind it, I came upon the small card I had earlier tucked into my waistcoat pocket.

LADY QUINCEBRIDGE
PYRE
HISLEY BEECHES
BERKSHIRE

HISLEY 25

Her troubled face peering through the window of the railway carriage came to my mind, and, sitting in my armchair, beside the fire, I thought calmly over her peculiar warnings and the forebodings she had expressed to me, but could still make no more sense of them than of those from other quarters, nor, in these safe, agreeable surroundings, take them at all seriously. But I resolved to accept her invitation for Christmas nevertheless, because I had liked her, and, I suppose, been flattered, as well as grateful, but more, because I felt that the time had come to enter at least some way into English society and begin to make myself known there.

I had always been a generally abstemious man but, that evening, drank a glass more port than was sensible, half-dozing before the heat of the fire, so that, when I stood to go to bed, I felt momentarily light-headed. But the bedroom was colder and I opened the window wide, and the smell of the fresh, snow-filled night air quickly brought me to my senses and cleared my head. As I leaned out a little way a thick seam of snow fell in a flurry far down into the yard below.

Not a light showed, the buildings around me were silent. The sky had cleared and there were bright stars.

My Guardian had sometimes spoken to me when I was a boy, about his Cambridge days, and I had formed a picture in my mind, augmented by engravings and pictures in books, of ancient walls and inner courts, quiet places devoted to learning and also echoing with the eager voices and swift steps of young men, and perhaps, though I was not a clever or very bookish boy, I had secretly begun to long for them and the longing had never quite left me, but remained, secret and half-forgotten. Now, it was stirred alive again, for I recognised that the school had many of the features of the old universities, and I stood for a long time looking down into the snow-covered yard, remembering my Guardian, happy to be at last a part of such a world.

As I undressed, I speculated about Dr Valentine Dancer, whom I was to meet the next morning, and about the pile of black notebooks on my desk, and what was to fill them, and felt anticipation and satisfaction in equal measure. It had been a good day. I had much to look forward to. I counted myself a fortunate man.

But then a chill breeze blew suddenly across the yard, and through my open window, and I shivered, and closed it, ready, now, for bed and sleep.

As I turned, a gleam of light struck the mirror on the opposite wall, and I looked up to face, as I thought, my own reflection. But there was none, there was nothing but a blurred, dark outline. Due, I supposed, to some trick of the atmosphere, the mirror was quite misted over. But, as I came up close to it, I saw quite clearly through the blur, my own eyes, staring, glittering, wild with a dread and alarm, terror even, that I was quite unaware of feeling. The bed was a wide one, neatly made, with pillows piled up high but when I slipped in between the tightly banded sheets they were cold, cold as winding sheets and felt like running water to my touch, though when I had turned them back they had felt quite crisp and dry. The pillows, as I sank back into them, collapsed with a little puff. Outside, the clock chimed the half-hour, a clear, double stroke, echoing towards me.

I lay shivering, and wide awake, and feeling nothing so much as a terrible sense of frustration and anger, that I was somehow to be forbidden peace of mind and pleasant expectations, that, whenever I was lulled and soothed and put at my ease by outward circumstances, I was then to be jerked out of that peace, my nerves were to be pulled taut as marionette strings, I was not allowed repose, but must be repeatedly startled and shocked into a state of fear and bewilderment and a sense of strangeness and dread by some slight but sinister and incongruous happening. I saw a pale, ragged boy, now here, now there, now following me, now a little ahead; I encountered hostility and was warned to leave, go back, beware. I was teased, I saw peculiar objects, and scenes that for no apparent reason awakened terror in me and made me want to run away, I heard singing and crying and then silence, in an empty house. The mirror had misted over.

I had been made so welcome, spent as serene and happy an evening in this place as I could have wished and then – I almost cried out in a sudden surge of desperation. I felt trapped, I did not know what was happening to me, or what I was meant to do.

Were the incidents linked, or quite random? Were they meaningless? Was I making connections where none existed? Had they meaning? Had anything? Were the phantoms and warnings and fearful moments brought about by anything outside myself, or was I losing my sanity? Was there nothing without, only things within?

I lay stiff between the icy sheets and heard the next hour chime and then another, and saw the pale snow-light reflected in the mirror, and the walls and the coverlet of the bed, and at last, calmer, told myself that the unaccustomed wine and tiredness had disturbed me and heated my blood, and so, believing, drifted to sleep.

But it was a restless and fretful one, wound about with veils of weird dreams. I seemed to be travelling, moving, wandering, unable to settle or find a way or distinguish anything that lay about me. I caught odd cries, then a

[69]

shout, I seemed to fall, to sweat, to be sinking down through dark, turbulent, sucking water – all the stuff of fever and nightmare.

When I woke, I was certain that, once again, a singing or crying had filled the room – or filled my head.

But there was only a sweet and peaceful stillness and silence and, beyond the half-drawn curtains, the falling snow. The clock chimed two. My mouth was cracked and dry, my throat sore. I wanted water and knew that I would not easily sleep again and did not want to lie there for hours, a prey to yet more dreams and fantasies, so that I rose briskly, dressed and went into the sitting room.

There was still a glow in the heart of the fire, which I had banked up, and I stirred it carefully to make a cavity, out of which soon came a lick of flame, and a little warmth. For a while, I sat, huddled, close beside it in the darkness, drinking a glass of water, and, gradually, I was composed again, the last trails of nightmare had loosened and dissolved away and I was returned to my old strength and even a feeling of vigour. It was curious, a repeat of what had happened before, as though, once out of some fit of nervousness and depression, I gained a fresh strength and command of myself again. I had never been prey to such complete and dramatic changes of mood and even of physical state. But, almost as if to prove to myself that I was man again, I decided to take a turn beyond my set of rooms, to explore some way down those corridors, gain a better sense of my surroundings. It could do no harm after all, no one would prevent me, and no sooner had I thought of the idea than I was full of it, restless, and almost excited, keyed up like a small boy, off exploring. I put on my overshoes and coat, mindful of the snow, should I venture outside the buildings, and, taking up the torch that had been provided for me, went quietly out, down the steep, short flight of stairs and through the door below, into the long, panelled corridor.

[70]

It was utterly silent. I stood still, sensing the walls and windows of the old buildings around me, and thought that I could almost hear the air itself as it settled back after I closed the door. Opposite me, the silvery light filtered through the leaded windows, set in their stone embrasures, and I noticed now that various large old books lay on the ledges. I opened one, and then others at random, but they were in Greek, Latin and Hebrew quite impenetrable to me, their pages musty and yellowing. I wondered how long it had been since anyone had last touched one.

The portraits that lined the walls were of little more interest – elderly men with sombre, hawk-like features, and bland clerics, though there were one or two frail, beautiful young men with flowing locks and mournful doe-eyes, poets who had been at Alton and died romantically young.

Though no one was there to see or hear me, I put out my torch and walked almost on tip-toe, cautiously, affected by the atmosphere and even half-amused at myself for such night-adventuring. I put my hand out to the latch of a couple of the other doors which I presumed led to similar sets to my own, but they were locked, as were those which sported the brass plates of Bursar, Chaplain, Provost.

I was losing interest and about to turn back, when I saw the door at the far end of the second long corridor – the Old Library – and at once made my way towards it.

It was as I was a few paces from the door that I began to have the sensation of being watched, watched and silently followed. I spun round and shone my torch behind me, for the windows had ended here and the corridor was pitch dark. There was no one. I went quietly back a few yards, stopped and waited, straining my ears through the silence. Perhaps the wood settled every now and again, perhaps a board creaked. Perhaps they did not. I waited again, and then said in a low voice, 'Who is there?' There was no reply and, impatient with myself and my imaginings, I turned back and went again to the library door.

I expected it to be locked, like the rest, but it swung open slowly to my touch, so that, involuntarily, I jumped back. The sensation of being watched was stronger and now my nerves were on edge and I cursed myself for a fool, not to have remained in my bed, where I would surely by now have been peacefully asleep. But my curiosity grew, for I was eager to examine the library, where I planned to be working for the next few days, and beginning to be fascinated by the grave, venerable beauty of this ancient place.

I stepped inside, and stood, letting my eyes grow accustomed to the change of light. I found myself in a room that stretched far ahead of me into the gloom. But there was enough of the soft, snow-reflected light coming in through the tall windows for me to have a view of a gallery, that ran the whole way around, rising towards the vaulted and elaborately carved ceiling. I felt no fear, but rather a sense of awe, as if I had entered some church or chapel.

Oak bookcases were lined on either side of the central aisle, with desks set in the spaces between, and as I looked up I could see more book stacks that rose behind the gallery, up to which iron spiral staircases led at intervals.

I went to a window, and saw that the library ran along the north end of the buildings framing the yard, at right angles to the chapel.

I turned away and began to walk softly between the bookcases, looking in awe to left and right, at the evidence of so much knowledge, so much learning, far beyond the level of school-age boys. I stopped to examine books on literature and the classics, the history of science, philosophy and theology, and then came upon rows of leather-bound archives of the school, magazines, journals, directories, lists. Somewhere within these, I knew, would be references to Vane, but I did not take out any now, I wandered on, with a growing and curious sense of being a king in some abandoned kingdom, with access to all the wisdom of the ages – such strange, grandiose thoughts flit into the mind under the influence of impressive surroundings, solitude, and the small hours.

It was as I approached the last few bays that I heard what at first I took to be the soft closing of the door at the far end of the room, but which went on, even and regular, like the breathing of someone asleep, a sighing that seemed to come out of the air above my head, as though the whole, great room were somehow a living thing, exhaling around me. I glanced up at the gallery. Someone was there, I was certain of it. The wood creaked. A footfall. I was as far from my way of escape as I could have been, trapped alone in this empty place with – whom? What?

'With nothing,' I said, aloud and boldly, scornfully – but then started at the sound of my own voice. 'Nothing.' And went to the spiral staircase nearest to me, and began to climb, my steps echoing harshly in the stillness of the room.

The gallery was dark, high and narrow, with only a foot or two of passage between the bookstacks, and the wooden rail. I switched off my torch. The air up here was colder, but at the same time oddly dead, and close, as though the dust of years, the dust of books and learning and thought, was packed tightly, excluding any freshness.

The soft breathing came again, from a different place, in the darkness just ahead of me and I began to edge forwards, and then to stop, move and stop, but it was always just out of reach. I looked down into the great barrel of the room below. Every shadow seemed like a crouched, huddled figure, every corner concealed some dreadful shape. There was no one there. There was nothing. There was everything. 'Who is there?' I said. 'What do you want of me?' Or would have said had not my throat constricted and my tongue cleaved to the roof of my mouth, so that no sound was possible. I wanted to run but could not and knew that this was what was intended, that I should be terrified by nothing, by my own fears, by soft breathing, by the creak of a board, by the very atmosphere which threatened me.

But, after a time of silence and stillness, I summoned up enough strength and steadiness of nerve to walk slowly, step by step, around the gallery, glancing down now and then but seeing nothing, until I came to the last staircase, and by that descended to the ground again. As I returned to the corridor, closing the door of the library behind me, I caught sight of a light moving about irregularly on the opposite side, and, as I rounded the corner, I glimpsed a dark-coated figure walking slowly, and holding up a lantern – the porter, I supposed, on his rounds, and felt a wave of relief so great that it all but felled me and took my breath, and I was forced to lean against the wall for a few seconds, so giddy did I become.

He it had been, watching me, following me, perhaps standing in the darkness of the library below, going about his duty, and suspecting prowlers, come, silently and stealthily, to investigate. Whether he had recognised or even seen me I could not be sure, but if so he had decided to leave me to look after myself and for that I was grateful – I felt somewhat sheepish at having gone about, trying doors, entering rooms without invitation, and I preferred to return quietly to my set and not be accosted.

He had gone off through the baize door, before I reached the bend in the corridor; I saw no more of his flickering light. All was quiet. The portraits looked down upon me blankly as I went by but I had no other sense of being seen.

And then I heard something else. It came from behind another door, an oak one set well back into the wall, with a green curtain pulled half across, and partially concealing it.

I stood up close to it and waited, listened. It came again, faintly, from somewhere deep within, and was quite unmistakable. What I heard was a boy weeping, the sobs now muffled slightly, now clear, as though he were raising and then burying his head again, and in between there was every so often a catching of breath, like a gasp, followed by more weeping. It was a sound so desolate, and of such loneliness and despair, that I felt outrage and anger and the urge to rescue him, to comfort, help, protect, and I put my hand to the door handle, ready to fling it open and burst in. But the lock did not give, the door was bolted and barred and, though I pushed against it and rattled the knob and even banged at it twice very hard, I made no impression, nor did I still the weeping, which continued without pause until I could bear it no longer. I could not break my way in to reach him, but there was someone who surely would.

I made off swiftly down the corridor towards the baize door. The snow lay thick, soft and undisturbed by any mark or footprint in the school yard, the surface gleaming faintly blue in the moonlight. It was intensely cold, the air crackling with frost. I was in such a state of anxiety about the distress of the hidden boy that for the moment I did not think anything about the pristine state of the snow, only plunged directly across it, sinking down and having to push my way forward with a great effort. I was breathless and desperate to find the porter – I would have to look for him first in the lodge, to which I prayed he had just returned – otherwise, he might be anywhere among these unfamiliar buildings, still on his night rounds.

The lodge was in darkness. I peered between cupped hands through the small windowpane, and saw that the fire had been banked up so that no glow or flame showed through.

I knocked twice, urgently, on the door, but then turned away and looked about me, trying frantically to plan which way I should go. I could not see the bobbing light, and the main gate by which I had first entered the school grounds was locked and barred. Where then? Where to go? My mind was confused. Until now, I had not so much as paused to ask who the boy might be; the school was down, he must be the child of some resident, a master or caretaker, I had no idea, and in any case it did not matter, he had been in such terrible distress, I had only the urge to reach and comfort him, rescue him from I knew not what. To my right lay the chapel, ahead the way to the cloisters and the upper corridor. I must go left then, take a chance that some door or passage would admit me to what the porter had called Scholars' House. But, as I pulled my coat collar up higher again and prepared to wade back across the snow, I heard a bolt being drawn in the door behind me and, turning, saw that the light had come on in the lodge.

'Sir? Mr Monmouth is it? You hammered fit to wake the dead.'

I stared. The porter stood before me, tousled and half-awake, an old waterproof pulled on over his nightshirt. It was quite clear to me that he had been asleep when I knocked a few minutes before.

'I'm sorry to disturb you when you have only just returned to bed – I would have hurried to catch up with you . . .'

'It is four o'clock in the morning, sir!'

And indeed, as he spoke, the clock in the tower began to chime, and in the distance, near and far, others sounded behind it through the cold still air. We were silent until the last strokes, and the echoes of them had died away and all was silent again.

'What did you think, sir?'

'Think?' I asked stupidly.

'The time, sir. That I should have only just gone to bed?'

I did not reply, and he looked at me with a patient smile.

'Four o'clock, sir,' he said again, as if to a small, dull child.

'I've been sound asleep these six hours past!'

As he spoke and I registered what he had said, I turned and looked at the single line of footprints across the snow and realised that they were my own and that there were no others, before me the snow had been quite undisturbed, no one else had come this way for hours – certainly not the porter, going steadily on his night rounds, carrying a lamp.

CHAPTER SEVEN

Dr Valentine Dancer was a man who matched his name. He was young, very lean, very slight, very bright, and he danced about on the balls of his feet a good deal as he spoke – indeed, he scarcely seemed able to stand still, but was now here, now there, dancing lightly as we went through the snow across the school yard.

It was a most glorious morning, the sky blue, the frost hard, the sun up, and he had arrived in my rooms as I was trying to make the best of the breakfast, brought to me by the porter after I had somehow slept through the last hours of a wretched night.

In the end, I had not told him about the crying boy, but only muttered that I had heard 'odd noises' along the corridor, and feared intruders. My nerves, I said, were not at all steady, after years living in remote and dangerous parts of the east. The man had given me an odd, sideways look.

'You're not used to the old buildings, sir, especially at night. It's easy to lose your nerve when alone. Now I am well used to it, sir, the odd creaks and bumps, none of it bothers me.'

'And that is all?'

'What exactly did you mean, sir?'

'There are only – odd creaks and bumps – nothing more – specific?'

'Not when the school is up, of course, sir, then there's all manner of them, sir – noises, I mean to say. Larks! But it's nice and quiet now, sir. You'd have been dreaming, that was it. Are you much given to dreaming, sir?'

He had walked back with me across the snow-covered yard and through the cloisters, his manner willing and cheerful, despite the hour, so that I felt quite myself again, only ashamed and rather foolish.

Now, we were at the door leading to my set.

'Now then, sir, here we are – quiet as a mouse. You'd have been dreaming, sir.'

'Yes. Yes, I suppose that I was. Thank you.'

'Goodnight again then, sir – or rather, good morning.'

'I do apologise.'

'Oh, I shall sleep again heavy enough, sir, don't you worry. *I* am not at all a man for dreaming.'

He had left me. I had not mentioned the sobbing, or the figure with the lamp. Both were gone, and I wanted to banish them from my thoughts too, wanted everything to be quiet and calm and normal, for what remained of the night.

He had not brought up my breakfast until just after ten o'clock, clattering the dishes and cutlery breezily, as I washed and dressed. The table was laid beside the window, from which I had a view of little more than sloping roofs, and the blue sky.

'No more snow, and a fine frosty morning, sir.'

'So I see. Thank you Biglow.'

He went off down the stairs whistling between his teeth, apparently none the worse for the disturbance of the night, and entirely forgiving of my strange behaviour.

I had no time to brood over those things however, and indeed had scarcely embarked upon my breakfast when I

[79]

heard light, bounding footsteps on the stairs and Dr Valentine Dancer made his entrance.

He had introduced himself, waited while I ate, and drunk a cup of tea and not for a moment been still. His face was fresh, and pink-cheeked from the cold air, his hair stuck up like the bristles of a brush and he wore an egg-yellow muffler wound around his neck many times and dangling down to his waist. I would have taken him for a keen office clerk or even an apprentice, for he did not have any of the gravitas of a schoolmaster and dean.

I had expected him to take me along to the library – and had made up my mind that I would not admit to having been into it already – show me the Vane archive, and leave me alone to get on with my work. Instead, he had suggested, moving about the room, darting to the window, prancing around me, that we go out for a tour of the school.

'The morning's so good, the air's as clean as a whistle – why frowst indoors? Plenty of time for that.'

I agreed gladly, pleased to have an opportunity of clearing my bleary head and eyes, and keen too, keen as one of the young schoolboys would have been, to be out in the snow.

As we walked, I looked closely at Dr Dancer. He had the curious, cheery look about him that is ageless – the face of an elderly infant, so that I could hazard no guess at how old he might really be. But, whatever his age, he proved to be an excellent, exuberant companion, tirelessly running up staircases, flinging open doors, crossing quads and playing fields, to show me classrooms, dormitories, drawing schools, gymnasiums, assembly hall, dining hall, another, more workaday library, all the offices of a huge school, and one such as I had never before seen.

And, as he explored, he talked; he was an inexhaustible mine of history, anecdote, legend, curious fact, about the place that was obviously his life, his hobby, his home, and his boundless enthusiasm. I was entertained, and interested, amused, and informed, but, above all, I was taken out of myself by this energetic little man.

At last we crossed a further playing field, went through a wicket gate and so out onto the towpath beside the River Thames. Dancer gestured to right and left. 'Boathouse. The weir. Are you an oarsman?'

'No, no.'

'Sportsman at all?'

'No. I played cricket and football of sorts at my mission school, many years ago. Nothing since.'

We were standing looking up river towards a graceful wooden bridge that curved across it to the opposite bank.

'If it gets much colder the river will freeze,' he said excitedly, 'and we shall have skating for Christmas.'

The bare branches of the willow trees, and the blades of tall grass and rushes, were iced white and stiff with frost. There was no wind, no sound at all save the rushing of the weir, and the cheeping, chattering sound made by a small party of coots and moorhens circling close to the bank.

'It is,' I said quietly, 'the most beautiful spot. It is perfect, it cannot be faulted.' I, who had travelled and seen such exotic sights, the glories of the world indeed, spoke the truth as I saw and felt it, most fervently.

'The bridge is particularly beautiful – the curve of it, the gentleness of the arch . . .'

'Ah – the haunted bridge!'

'The . . .'

He chuckled and seemed to do a little jig at my side.

'We have two ghosts at Alton – perfectly friendly and harmless, the pair of them. The shadowy man in grey who crosses this bridge at dusk, and the servant laying places at table in Scholars' Hall. Though neither, I think, have been sighted lately. Perhaps you will be lucky!'

We walked on, and mounted the bridge. The wooden boards were slippery with frost, so that I almost fell and Dancer had to grab my arm. Then, leaning on the rail and looking at the glittering surface of the water, I said lightly, 'And are there really no other ghosts, in such an ancient place?'

'None. Odd, you will agree. But none. It is a good, a happy place. It has always been so – for the most part.'

I said nothing.

'It quite disappoints the boys. They'd love some good midnight groaning and clanking of chains. Bloodthirsty creatures, boys.'

'Yes.'

'So you have nothing to worry about, Mr Monmouth.'

I saw that he was looking very closely at me, and that, for the first time, he was also standing absolutely still.

I wanted to tell him, I had a tremendous urge to unburden myself, beginning not with the events of the previous night, but going back to the evening I had arrived in England. And I might indeed have spoken, but, at that moment, there was an eerie noise from up river, and looking in that direction we saw a flock of wild geese bearing down upon us, honking as they went, and the sound grew louder and mingled with the leathery clapping of their great wings. Dancer and I watched entranced, turning to follow them as they disappeared round the bend in the river. 'What a sight that is!' He was on the move again, bobbing up and down with excitement.

It was cold and we began to move off the bridge.

'We'll walk up river. We can see the line of the buildings to such good effect from here. The chapel looks best of all,' Dancer said, as proudly as if he were master of the place.

I went along beside him, looking where I was bid, listening again.

I did not speak of anything, after all.

He ended our tour outside a row of houses set behind neat front gardens, behind Scholars' House.

'Bachelor masters live in the boarding houses, or rooms

in the High Street, some senior masters in the cloisters. But . . .' he flung open the front gate with a grand gesture, 'we married men live here!'

A door stood open, and in the doorway a little huddle of solemn children, all with the red-cheeked, gnome-like face of Dr Dancer. Behind them was a tall young woman carrying an infant. We went up the path.

'Hetty, my wife – Mr James Monmouth, our visitor.' He then extended his arm to the young ones. 'And Evelyn – Isaac – Japhet, and – ' here, he swept the baby out of his wife's arms – 'Hector,' he concluded with a flourish.

I was ushered into his study, a young maid brought tea, the children were banished. It was a handsome room overlooking lawns and bare cedar and elm trees, with the open playing fields beyond. Books lined the walls, mainly, I saw, works of history, and a fire burned in the grate. His desk was piled high with papers.

'I have everything a man could wish for, and the best of all, Monmouth, is that I know it, I know it. Happy that man!'

Coming from any other, it would have sounded intolerably smug but I could only smile, warming even more to Dancer, disarmed by his innocent pride and pleasure in his life, and work, his family and his situation.

'You will stay to lunch, of course,' he said, 'though I fear it will be a bear garden. Still, they must stare their fill of you and ask you every question under the sun and then they will have had enough and leave you be.'

'It is very good of you to be so hospitable and I am extremely grateful, but . . .' I set down my teacup, 'the fact is, I am very anxious to go into the library and be shown the Vane papers so that I may begin work at once.'

Dancer stopped swivelling in his chair. The room was silent. His face was serious now, and wary.

'Plenty of time for that,' he said.

[83]

'No, Dr Dancer, there is not. I cannot intrude upon the school and take your hospitality for granted for too long.'

'Oh, we are perfectly happy to have you, perfectly . . .'

'Nevertheless, I wish to get down to work.'

'So be it then. I will take you directly after lunch.'

He got up and went to the window, hands clasped behind his back. From elsewhere in the house, I heard muffled roars of rage, then running footsteps. Laughter, the banging of a door.

'I take it,' I said calmly, 'that you, too, are about to use your best efforts to deter me from the work I propose to begin.'

After another few, silent moments, he came back to his chair, but again sat very still, staying any movement with his feet upon the floor.

'What do you know of Conrad Vane?'

Briefly, and somewhat wearily, too, for I had answered the question before, I told him.

'Oh yes, yes, all that, the travels, the exploration – all that was perfectly in order, so far as I know. Admirable even, in its way.'

'But then . . .'

'All that came much later, at the end of his life. It was incidental, it did not make up for the man, nor for what went before.'

I waited for him to continue.

'Do you know why you are so intent upon pursuing your interest in the man, what it is about him that so fascinates you?'

'No, I confess to you that I do not, it is a mystery, a puzzle. But from many years ago, when I first read of him, in a book in my late Guardian's library, I was strangely drawn to him and the fascination – for you are right, that is exactly what it is – has never waned, indeed, I have felt myself to be more and more in thrall to it.'

'To have come under his spell?'

[84]

I shrugged.

'There is a power, an attraction, exerted by evil . . .'

'Oh come!'

'Yes, evil. Others have found themselves drawn by it – magnetised, as they were in his lifetime. Conrad Vane was an evil man, Monmouth, evil and depraved, and he used the power of wickedness, a dreadful power, over others, the innocent, the naive, the immature, the foolish. I have read, and I have heard some of the stories and investigated them, to my own satisfaction. It was enough.'

'And what are these stories? What did he do?'

'He was cruelty personified – the stories are of that and of corruption of the innocent as well as more ordinary, unpleasant human traits – spitefulness, deceit, brutality, debauchery, viciousness, cunning. It began when he was a boy – no, perhaps it began at or even before his birth, and, in the end, he was obliged to go abroad and, I daresay, pursue his evil career among other devils.'

'I cannot believe we are talking of the same man – Vane, the great explorer, the sensitive chronicler of places – peoples and their customs . . . the solitary adventurer.'

'I agree. From what I have discovered, there did indeed seem to be two, very contrasting sides to the man – Jekyll and Hyde, no less.'

I tried to make sense of what Dancer was telling me. Beyond the windows, blackbirds pecked at the frozen grass. The sky above the trees was almost silver. A beautiful morning. A perfect day.

'I am grateful to you,' I said at last. 'I have received hints, and veiled warnings. No one has begun to speak the truth until now.'

He smiled and began, very gently, to swivel his chair round again.

'So I have deterred you,' he said, 'I am profoundly glad of it. Now, you will stay to enjoy lunch.'

'No, Dr Dancer, you have told me things, but you have

made no difference, you have not deterred me. Why would I be deterred?'

His face was not so much serious as sad.

'You have whetted my appetite even further. My fascination is keener still.'

He groaned.

'What a subject!' I went on. 'What contrasts, what a host of extraordinary contradictions – what questions it raises! I scarcely know where to begin. I am unable to believe my luck. I shall in the end present the portrait, the study, of a very rare man indeed before the public.' I was becoming carried away by what I was saying.

'There is more,' Dancer said.

'Ah, yes, the warnings! Beware!'

'The power of evil to do harm is very real, very strong.'

'I have no doubt of it.'

'Many suffered.'

'Dancer, the man is dead!'

'And does that mean that it has ended there?'

'Oh come, man!'

My words were brave, I heard my own voice, blustering, full of scorn. But they were hollow and I was trembling within.

Dancer was looking at me as if he were weighing something up, deciding whether or not to speak.

'Well, what is it?'

He shook his head.

'What is your own interest in Vane?' I asked sharply.

'None. I have none. Once, I read a little, out of idle curiosity. After I had heard rumours, I began to delve into such archive as the school possesses. I discovered enough to make me retreat, to retreat and close the books and turn my back. Vane was acclaimed a great man by some, after his death. Well, perhaps, in some ways, he became one. He ventured where no man had previously dared to venture, discovered much. But he was also a liar, a time-server, a bully, a cheat and worse. He lived as he wished, he had his way, at the expense of others, because it pleased and amused him to do so, because it helped him to achieve his own ends, because he was corrupt and in love with power. That is how he obtained satisfaction. When he was forced to leave this country for his evil doings, he went abroad and swaggered there. He used and abused the ignorant and the innocent, though all the while he showed a face of honeyed sweetness to the world. Is this the man in whose company you would spend your hours? Your time alone? Leave him, Monmouth, let him rot.'

He shuddered suddenly, and got up and began to pace about the room, rubbing his hands together in agitation.

'You speak almost as if you had known him, as if he had done you personal harm.'

'Not I,' he said. 'Others.'

He faced me again. 'Let him lie. Do not open the book.'

'I am grateful to you, as I have said. I understand more now, much more. But I would ask you to trust me to read further for myself. I cannot leave it there and be so easily deterred, without proving things to myself at least.'

'You are a stubborn man.'

Yes. In this matter I seemed to have become one, to be gripped by a force outside myself, an urge to go and penetrate to the heart of the mystery, and stare into it with my own eyes. I had never known such a determination, unless it had been at those times when I had passionately wanted to journey into some unknown region, some danger, following in Vane's footsteps. I was aware that in this matter, as in no other, I was not myself. I was almost like a man possessed.

Then Dancer said, his voice almost a whisper, 'Whoever touches, explores, follows after Vane, will be run mad, and will never afterwards rest his head or enjoy his peace or have a home. He will be haunted. He will be cursed. I saw what lay ahead, Monmouth. I drew back.'

A door opened. I heard the infant laughing, a soft, innocent laugh.

I looked at Dancer. 'But,' I said, at last, and realised the
stark truth even as I spoke it, 'unlike you, I have nothing at
all to lose.'

CHAPTER EIGHT

Dancer's manner changed. As soon as he understood, by my quiet determination, that I intended to continue with my plans no matter what, he dropped his solemn manner, and any attempt to prevent me, and became relaxed again and even cheerful, albeit in a slightly more restrained way than before. It was as though a shadow had fallen and an invisible barrier been set up between us, and for that I was sorry. I liked the man, and I wanted to retain his friendship – it might be that, in the days to come, I would need it.

I did not stay at his house for lunch. Instead, Dancer took me back through the schoolyard towards the cloisters, a quieter man now, no longer chatting about our surroundings, but, instead, telling me as much as he knew about the references to Conrad Vane that would be available to me.

'I hope you will not be disappointed, and feel your visit here has been fruitless,' he said. 'What you will find is very dull stuff, lists and so forth – nothing out of the way at all, perhaps nothing to suit your purpose.'

I did not believe him, but I replied, 'Perhaps not, but I have to make a start and this is the best place to do so. I daresay it will lead me elsewhere very soon.'

'Possibly, possibly.'

He darted ahead of me, to open the baize door at the top of the steps. The panelled corridor was cool and dim but some sunlight came shafting through here and there, picking up the motes of dust which spun about within them.

'I imagine there is rather more in the way of bustle and activity here, during the school term.'

'A little, though the boys do not come here of course.'

'Never?'

'Not unless they're in trouble! A senior boy might visit a tutor from time to time, but for the most part it retains its hushed and learned atmosphere.'

'Do no families live here?'

'No – as I said, we married men are housed in King's Walk.'

We were reaching the end of the corridor. The library was ahead.

I wanted to ask directly about the crying boy, and dared not. As we came up to it, I could not restrain myself from looking left at the recessed oak door, behind which I had heard his desperate sobbing.

It was not there.

I stopped dead.

'Is something wrong?' Dancer was looking back at me with concern. He had taken out a bunch of keys and was sorting through them. I did not reply, but turned and walked slowly back, the whole way along the corridor, to the corner, and the entrance to my own rooms. Then I retraced my steps. Every other door was as I had recalled, and seen it, the brass plates there, as before. Only the dark door behind the half-drawn curtain was not.

Dancer was staring at me.

'My dear man, are you unwell? You are deathly pale.'

I took several deep breaths, trying to steady myself. I did not want to tell him anything.

He watched me, grave-faced.

'It is nothing. I am subject to these moments of faintness

– giddiness – they are alarming to others but do not bode
any ill, they are not at all serious. I daresay that it is merely
a mild, inherited weakness.' I heard myself, babbling on.

'Very well.'

He did not pursue the matter, but turned back to the
library door, continuing to search through his keys.

'I have so many, there are so many doors in this place. If
I have mislaid it, I shall have to step back and find Droggett, he will let us in.'

'Perhaps,' I said cautiously, 'the door will be unlocked.'

'No, no, the library is never left open, there are some very
rare and valuable things. We have never surprised any
thieves, but terrible damage could be caused by some accident, and the loss would be incalculable.'

Yet the library door had been open the previous night.

'Ah!' He selected a key. 'It is very similar to two others.'

Now he would find it open. I supposed that the porter
had been careless and would be in trouble for it.

Dancer was bending. 'There – it is always a little stiff
when no one has been in for a day or two.' He gave a sharp
twist of his hand and pressed down. For a second, the lock
held and then gave. I heard a click and the key turned.
Dancer opened the door.

The library was exactly as I had seen it the previous night,
and quite empty. We stepped inside and he surveyed it,
swept his hand round in an expansive gesture. 'This is one
of the most ancient parts of the school, as old as the chapel.
It is known as the Old Library, to distinguish it from the
school library, but also as The King's Room – it was established by him. There are documents actually relating to
King Henry, deeds, a royal charter – they are kept in strong
boxes in the muniment room alas, and I do not have access
to them. But I can show you other treasures . . .'

By the time I had followed him around the room for
some fifteen minutes, I had recovered my composure and

although I did not take in much of what he was saying I looked, with as great a show of interest as I could muster, as he opened cupboards and lifted up glass display cases, pulled out books, showing me the library's most rare and precious volumes as proudly as if he himself were owner of them. Every so often, he shot me a keen glance but for the most part he was so carried away with excitement and enthusiasm that I might not have been there and did not need to do more than admire, as I was bid.

But at last he closed an early printed book, scattered with fine woodcuts of martyrs, snapped shut the brass clasp that bound it, and said, 'Now – Vane. The archive is over here,' and led me briskly back down the room to the shelves I had begun to examine the night before – if indeed I had, if the door had indeed been open, if I had not been dreaming.

But they were as I had seen them, the leather-bound school journals and records, row after dull row. I had been here.

Dancer went briskly about other bays, and twice up to the stacks in the gallery, as well as to some cupboards at the far end of the library, returning with piles in his arms, travel journals, volumes of letters, geography, a history of the school.

'Anything by Vane, or which mentions him – and there is really very little and much of it will be quite without interest – it is all here.'

He stacked the books on a table in a window bay. Others were piled around it on the floor.

I looked out. The tall windows gave onto the gardens leading down to the towpath and the river. I could see the curve of the wooden bridge, and I let my eye rest upon it, a firm, sure thing, spanning the sparkling water, it was a scene which I wanted to hold before my eyes as long as I could, for reassurance, for I had begun to feel that I might be slipping gradually and uncontrollably into some uncertain nightmare world, where things changed and shifted, and I could no longer trust to my own senses.

I realised that Dancer was waiting beside me, silently.

'Thank you,' I said hurriedly, 'it is very good of you to go to so much trouble and, now I have everything I could possibly need, I will simply get down to work at once. I don't want to take up any more of your time.'

'You will find paper and writing materials, everything of that sort, in these drawers. If there is anything else . . .'

'Indeed, yes. Thank you.'

'We are always available to you – you are to come to us – you must not hesitate – join us, for meals, conversation – I do not want to think of you here too much alone.'

It was a welcome invitation and one that comforted me. I thanked him again, assured him that I accepted it in advance for whenever the need or desire for his company and that of his family should arise.

He left me, his brisk footsteps going off down the corridor, out of my hearing. The library was quite silent. I listened intently, but the breathing sound had gone. I stood on at the windows, looking out for a little longer at the sunshine on snow, and, as I looked, I saw a little line of people, and realised that they were Dancer's wife, together with a young girl I took to be the nursemaid, and the children. They were going slowly towards the bridge, the little boys scuffling about and throwing snowballs – I could see them laughing and calling out, see their bright, rosy, upturned faces, their gleeful expressions, though I could hear nothing at all, they were too far below. The woman had set the baby down now and was urging it to walk a step or two, but it stood uncertainly, wobbled, and then plonked down in a flurry of snow, and the others crowded around it, laughing and prancing in delight, and it seemed to me then that the glorious morning, the sunshine, the snow, the blue sky and the beautiful old buildings all around, with the river beyond, were a sort of happy paradise and they enjoying it in their young innocence. But I was not part of it, I was excluded, and could only look on, sealed away behind the high windows in the room above.

I worked my way steadily through the books for about three hours with scarcely a pause, save for one trip back to my rooms to fetch overcoat and scarf – for it was very cold in the library, though Droggett appeared after a time with a bucket of glowing coals, to light a small iron stove that stood on a stone hearth in one corner. But the amount of heat that it gave out was pitiful indeed, and my fingers became white and stiff and I fumbled clumsily with the pages. But no one else disturbed me and there were no strange noises, not so much as the creaking of a board. I refused to allow my mind to contemplate the matter of the vanished door and the locked library, preferring to get on with the work in hand and tell myself that I had been hallucinating.

I found that Dancer had been right, the records were mainly uninteresting. I found Vane's school dates and information about which had been his house, saw his name in one or two sports teams of the lower divisions, discovered that he had been a rowing coxswain and so forth. On first coming across his name, I felt a slight spurt of excitement, but that soon faded as I ploughed on without anything of greater interest coming to light. It was clear that, for his first two or three years at least, Conrad Vane had had an all-but-anonymous school career, in common with many hundreds of other unmemorable boys.

I glanced at the printed travel journals and other books of descriptive writings. They included Vane's own three published works, and two or three essays which he had contributed to others, but there was nothing I did not already own, and had read many times. Other books covered much the same ground, and were written by men with whose names I was familiar, including two of those spoken of by Beamish, the bookseller. They mentioned Vane, but only in passing, and in a few he was merely referred to in a footnote.

I began to feel dispirited. I also wondered if Dancer had kept anything back from me.

Beyond the window, the light became grey as the afternoon wore on and the sun went behind the buildings. Once or twice I looked out, noting each time how the river changed from steel to black and that shadows fell across the snow, dulling its surface.

A few times, I paced up and down the long room in an effort to warm myself, and stood up close to the little stove, rubbing my hands. I did not want to eat, I simply read on and on in the peace of the old library, and felt no disturbance in the atmosphere around me, nor had any sense of being observed. All was remarkably tranquil and steadying to the nerves for most of that afternoon.

It was after two o'clock by the time I came to the first hint of anything of more than fleeting interest – a record of a senior school debate. It was upon the subject of Voodoo and Witchcraft, and 'a prominent and vociferous speaker' had been C.P.R. Vane. Shortly after that, in a copy of a magazine written and produced by some boys, I found notice of the proposed foundation of The Cloven Hoof Club, 'a Private Society for investigation, discussion and experiment', signed C.P.R.V. It sounded like nothing more than a schoolboy attempt to shock, to seem important, mysterious and wicked, without much real harm. I was made more uneasy by a notice, some months later, in the official school Record, that upon the order of the High Master, Dr Birdlip, the Club had been disbanded, and all its activities and any meetings between its former members proscribed.

So – Vane had dabbled in the occult, like many a stupid young man before and after him. It made him a fool, and an unpleasant one too, but I wondered if any of the tales and rumours I had been told amounted to more than gossip that had gathered colour over the years, and stories that had grown more alarming with every re-telling.

I went on turning the pages of the Record, fascinated by the picture it painted of the life of the school half a century before, wondering how much things had changed, discovering small items of interest, such as the fact that Dancer's father had been Dean, before him, but this was the last volume I intended to peruse that day, for it had grown even colder, the afternoon was drawing in and darkening, and I fancied hot tea and toast, before my fire.

And then I came upon first the report, in the Record, and then, clipped to its page, the account taken from a newspaper, of the death of a boy at Alton. His body had been found, hanging from a beam in a locked room. He had been beaten, and it was stated that, when last seen, and for some days previously, he had appeared to be in a state of distress. He was thirteen years old and his family resided at Kittiscar Hall, in the remote village of the same name in North Yorkshire.

His name was George Edward Pallantire Monmouth.

CHAPTER NINE

In the middle of the night, I remembered the leather trunk.

I woke from an exceptionally deep and quite dreamless sleep into the soft snow-reflected light of the bedroom, and, as I did so, I had a clear picture in my mind of the shabby brown trunk, with domed lid and iron handles, which contained everything I had kept from the things in my Guardian's bungalow in Africa. He had not hoarded possessions, and by the time I had cleared out, and given away the everyday domestic stuff, there had been mainly books left, together with a few treasures he had collected over his nomadic life, and some personal items I had not felt it right to part with. Immediately after his death I had gone very thoroughly through his papers, partly out of necessity, in order to clear up any business affairs, but also in the hope of finding something relating to myself, some small clue as to my parentage and background. There had been nothing. It was as though I had come newly into the world when I arrived here at the age of five, and had had no previous existence. Whether he had deliberately destroyed any papers I did not know, and, as soon as I saw that there was nothing, I had ceased to trouble myself about the matter; I had simply packed up what I wanted, or thought ought to be kept, and stored the trunk, along with a few things of my own, in a vault in the city some miles away. There they had remained until I had begun to make my arrangements to return to England. Now, the trunk stood, still strapped and undisturbed, together with the rest of my belongings that had been delivered by the shipping company to Number 7, Prickett's Green.

I did not know why it should now have come quite so vividly into my mind, but I lay and thought about the trunk, looked at it, as it were, in my imagination, unstrapped it and lifted the lid, but I could not recollect very much about what it contained, for I remembered little about that time. I only knew that I had to sort through everything anew, for I was even more desperate to find some trace of my former existence.

George Edward Pallantire Monmouth. Was it the purest and most bizarre coincidence that he bore my own surname? Had he anything whatsoever to do with me?

I would not rest until I had found out. In my heart, I was certain there must be some connection, that that was why I had been so driven by my intense interest in Conrad Vane. I believed that, in some way, my family had had dealings with him, and that the dead boy had some connection with me.

Was it his poor ghost that I had heard sobbing behind the door? Was he the pale boy? Had he been trying to attract my attention, haunting me in a desperate effort to seek my help? And what did he want? Peace? Succour? Or vengeance? All things seemed possible, that night, things I had never before dreamed of as likely, but would always have dismissed out of hand. My recent experiences had begun to open my mind, but it had not been until I had come here to Alton, read what I had read yesterday afternoon, and begun to uncover the truth about Conrad Vane, and above all seen the name, George Edward Pallantire Monmouth, set out before me, that I had been fully convinced of things that lay out of sight, below the surface of the ordinary world.

Strangely, I was less afraid than I had been. I no longer thought that I was ill or mad, or the butt of some malicious trick.

It was bitterly cold in the room. Ice had formed delicate and beautiful leaf and fern patterns on the inside of the windows. But it was quiet, the atmosphere felt as tranquil and undisturbed as it had been all day. I had spent the evening staring into the fire, trying to make some sense of what I had found, and recover from the shock I had received. There had been no incidents, no spirits of good or evil had sought me out. It was as though, by touching upon the truth, I had vanquished them, or else laid them to rest. I hoped that they would not return. But I did not intend to leave the matter, I could not, not now, I would have to get to the heart of it. If nothing else, I must satisfy myself about the boy. Moreover my interest in Vane had changed. At first, I had planned to write some eulogistic biography of a hero. Then, as I had discovered more, to present the portrait of a fascinating, strangely divided character, to the world. I wanted both to expose and explain him. But now, in beginning to find out about Vane, I had apparently stumbled upon clues to my own history, and I cared about this most passionately of all. If the two were in some way intertwined, then I meant to unravel the threads.

I returned to London the following day. When I went across to the house to tell Dancer, he seemed surprised and also considerably relieved.

'I am afraid that I am not taking your advice,' I said. 'But I have made a discovery – something I would prefer to keep to myself, and this makes it imperative for me to return to London.'

'Then your visit to Alton has not been fruitless – the records were of some interest?'

'Yes.'

He searched my face. 'You seem calm,' he said, 'untroubled.'

'Entirely.'

'I pray that you will remain so.'

I thanked him, and then asked if he knew whether there had been any alterations to the corridor above the cloisters at any time. I thought that he looked wary.

'Not in recent years. As I told you, that is the oldest part of the school, and in a way rather separate from it. Elsewhere there have been changes – the boys' living quarters were somewhat medieval and lacking in comfort, they have been improved greatly, even since I was a scholar here.'

'I would be glad if you could spare the time to come with me,' I said. 'There is something I want to reassure myself about in your presence.'

As we went through the baize door leading to the upper corridor I paused. 'Take note,' I said, 'of all the doors. I will count them as we go along.'

I did so, numbering them aloud or else reading out from their brass plates, Bursar – Muniment Room – Provost – they were exactly as I had first seen them. As we walked along, I saw that Dancer's face was clouded, his manner wary.

I stopped. 'Here,' I said.

He glanced at me, and then at the wall to which I was pointing.

'What is there?' I asked.

'Why nothing – a blank wall,' he replied.

'And behind?'

'I have no idea what you mean.'

'Was there never a door? Might there be a room behind here?' I touched the wall.

'There is no way in to any room. Unless, of course, some store lies behind here, to which entrance might be gained from within.'

'Via an inner passage?'

'I really cannot remember the exact arrangement – this is a very ancient building as you know, a veritable rabbit warren of passages and rooms.'

I was silent. There was a blank wall before us, that much was clear. I ran the flat of my hand across it, but there was not even a slight alteration in the texture or level of the plaster that might have indicated a blocked-up door.

'Nothing,' I said.

Yet I was loath to leave – leave him, as it seemed, immured somewhere, sobbing and despairing of any help or comfort.

George Edward Pallantire Monmouth.

His crying echoed in my head.

I turned and almost ran from that haunted place.

At Alton, the snow had been a thing of beauty, to be admired, and enjoyed, a foil to the ancient stone buildings, and softening the landscape all about me.

But London was a city paralysed by winter, frozen to its heart, the pavements rutted and treacherous, the roads a mire of sugary brown slush. In squares and gardens where the snow still lay untrampled, save by the claws of a million birds, it could perhaps be looked upon with pleasure, but going about one's business, even walking a short way, cold and stumbling, was misery indeed. Only the glow of braziers from workmen's huts and chestnut and hot potato stalls warmed and brightened the dark, and made fragrant the air that seemed black with frost and tasted bitter on the tongue.

From my windows, I looked out over the half-frozen river and cabs and struggling passers-by, and my fire gave out no warmth, and the winter and the whiteness quite lost their charm for me. And everywhere, it seemed, I now saw only the cold and homeless and half-starved poor, wretches huddled in corners, shivering, and ragged, as though the bitter weather had somehow brought them to light, exposed them and left them stranded like flotsam at low tide. I was more conscious of this dark side of London than at any time since my arrival in the city.

But I did not spend much time contemplating it, nor sit as I had previously done, for hours in the window, enjoying the life of the river beyond.

I had thrown my bag unopened on the bed, cast off my coat, and, after stirring the fire into meagre life, dragged the old leather trunk out from its standing place in the passage and fumbled with the stiff clasps and locks that had bound it and been untouched for more than twenty years.

For the rest of that day, and halfway through the night, I was deaf and blind to all else save its contents and when finally, with red-rimmed eyes and breaking back, I was forced to abandon it and stagger to bed, I slept – still half-dressed – going over the piles of books and belongings in my dreams, before rising to continue my search, as the dawn came up.

For a long time, I found nothing, though I opened and flicked through every book, ripped apart every envelope, read every letter. The past, and my life as a boy and young man, growing up in my Guardian's care in Africa, was gradually laid out on the floor as I unpacked the trunk, but for the time being I held back the memories. Later, perhaps, I could afford to give them rein, see and hear and live again that calm and happy time. Not now, now I was in a fever of mind to find something that would let me through another door into a different and wholly forgotten life.

From time to time, I paused to take a turn about the room; went once to the coffee house, where I sat in a daze, exhausted and scarcely noticing what it was that I ate and drank; I threw more coals onto the fitful fire and, eventually, got up a decent blaze. The sky beyond the windows was fiery orange, as the afternoon drew in, and later on it darkened, the frost seemed to smoke off the surface of the water.

The building below me was utterly empty and silent still, the stairs had been in darkness as I came up. Threadgold had appeared, muttering morosely at my return, but soon retreated again to his secret basement.

Once, I heard the fire engine's frantic bell, and saw light blazing out from a house further along the walk, heard distant shouting. I switched on the lamps. It grew quiet again, as if the world outside my windows had been frozen into motionless silence by the intensity of the cold.

I found no letter, no documents relating to me, no birth certificate – which surely my Guardian must once have had – no reference at all to my existence. If there had been any papers, they had been destroyed.

Light-headed with disappointment and fatigue I began to feel like a wraith myself, it was as though I had no substance, no real existence in this world at all.

And, then, I came upon the Prayer Book.

It was a small copy, bound in soft black, with wafer-thin pages. I riffled through it, shaking it, as I had with every one of the books in the trunk, in case some slip of paper should be inside. Nothing fell. But, as I closed it, my eye caught the line of writing inside the front cover. It was in dark ink, still strong and clear because it had not been exposed to the light,

James Monmouth
His, to remember Old Nan

Kittiscar 18-

I stared at the careful, old-fashioned handwriting, stared until I might almost have burned the words off the paper, and as I stared something deep within me stirred in response, but just out of reach so I could not grasp it – a name, a place, a time, a person, a voice – what? What? I almost sobbed with frustration, knowing yet not knowing, I felt like a man blindly running down twisting tunnels, swerving, stretching out my hands to grasp what lay ahead and hold it to me, shake it, bid it yield up its secret.

Old Nan. Old Nan.

I flung myself into the chair, and remained there, as the fire sank and slumped down upon itself, my brain straining frantically, scouring every recess of my memory.

Old Nan.

There it was! Yes, I had it . . . there . . . No. A hint, then, a slight scent, faintly, in my nostrils. Then it was gone again.

Old Nan.

But I was satisfied in one respect.

George Edward Pallantire Monmouth, of Kittiscar Hall, Kittiscar.

I had proved his connection with me.

I slept in the chair that night, beside the dying fire, and woke in the early hours of the morning cold as death, my head aching, so that I cried out in pain when I moved, and, when I stood, was giddy. All around me, the contents of the trunk lay in piles, books, papers, little half-opened packages of this and that. But the one book, the only thing I cared for, or which held any interest for me, was still clutched between my fingers, as it had been all that night.

James Monmouth.
His, to remember Old Nan

Kittiscar, 18-

CHAPTER TEN

The following morning, I received a letter from Lady Quincebridge reminding me of my engagement to spend Christmas with them, and stating that, unless she heard to the contrary, she would have me met from the three o'clock train at Hisley, on Saturday, Christmas Eve.

From what I had seen of her, and from the nature of her address and invitation, I thought it likely that the house would be a grand one and the party smart, and that I should therefore need to get myself a few more clothes. For the next couple of days, therefore, I was too busy to do anything more – even supposing I knew what more might be done – about pursuing the information I had found written inside the Prayer Book.

I went to a modest gentlemen's outfitters off Piccadilly, and purchased a dinner suit, smoking jacket, and a new, heavy overcoat, together with various extras in the way of respectable dressing gown and slippers, shirts and shoes. I might even have enjoyed making my purchases, had I not felt tired and somewhat out of spirits, with a vague aching in my limbs and head, which I did my best to ignore.

A thaw set in just before Christmas Eve, so that the streets and roadways turned to rivers of black, frothing water. The sky was overcast, the air foul, and it scarcely seemed to come light all day. But I went for a walk among the stalls of Covent Garden market, and enjoyed the sights and smells, of fresh, piled Christmas trees and mounds of bitter-smelling holly, the geese, turkeys and capons swinging in rows outside butchers' doorways, fetched down every so often by aproned boys bearing hooked wooden poles.

The previous Christmas, I recalled, I had spent in a remote mountain village in Tibet, drinking rancid buttered tea and listening to the eerie chants of the Buddhist monks and the tinkling of a thousand bells, across the thin, pure air. It had been as far from this murky London mire and coming Christian festival as might have been, another world, a dream – I could scarcely believe in it.

When I returned to Prickett's Green that night to pack my belongings, I still felt somewhat depressed and thought that I might have caught a chill, but I took some powders, with hot rum, slept well, and, in the morning, a sluggish, dark, raw one, decided that I had succeeded in shaking it off before it took hold.

I dressed with some care, locked up the rooms – I had left a note for Threadgold, who was, as usual, invisible – and called a cab to take me to Waterloo. At the last minute, I slipped the small black Prayer Book into my pocket.

It was a gloomy journey, the railway train was crowded, and I ill-tempered with my fellow-passengers. I retreated into myself, hunched into my corner, and brooded, turning the inscription in the book over and over in my mind, trying yet again to catch and pin down those hints of something, something that I knew, and which would open the door into my past for me. But I was no more successful than before and almost began to wish that I had not found the book and so had nothing to tantalise me, nothing to pursue.

I realised that Conrad Vane, and what I had discovered

about him, had ceased to dominate my thinking – indeed now I recoiled from the very thought of him. My attitude was quite changed. It was the boy, George Edward Pallantire Monmouth, to whom I was now in thrall.

The train rattled on and my brain seemed to rattle with it. I was in a half-daze, half-dream, and only woke with a start because the carriage seemed suddenly so stiflingly hot I was forced to fling off my coat and jacket to cool myself, though my fellows stared at me hard enough, for doing so.

The countryside beyond the windows was dull and drear, rain slashed across from the west, and mournful animals stood about, heads bowed, in the waterlogged fields. For the first time since my arrival, I longed for the heat of the tropics, for blue skies and vivid flowers, bright-ness, the glare of the sun and the huge open continent stretching away from me on every side, I felt cramped and oppressed, I had no purpose here, I lacked friends, and all those I saw around me had closed, dull, pallid faces.

At Hisley, I was met by a car, a dark green Bentley, and I sat back in the deep upholstery, my bags stored away in the boot, willing myself to enjoy the luxury, but apprehensive, sure I had far better have remained at Prickett's Green, mouldering alone over a fire, for I felt uncertain as to how I might be received and whether I would be at my ease and not entirely out of place in some grand house among strangers, with a hostess I barely knew. But the car turned in through a pair of high gates and in spite of my forebod-ings I sat forward to look ahead for my first sight of Pyre. As if aware of my interest and to make the most of the approach, the chauffeur slowed the car. The rain had stopped and the sky cleared and lightened a little, though it was still a dull enough day and drawing in rapidly. After a short drive between uninteresting shrubs we swung round into a long, straight carriage ride between great elms, with parkland on either side, in which small deer were grazing. I imagined it in high summer, with the leafy branches meeting in an arch overhead and the sunlight filtering through the leaves. This was the England of which I had read in the stories in my Guardian's books when I was a boy; this was the sort of picture I had carried for years in my mind.

'Now you see the house, sir, there, ahead.'

I looked and, as I saw it, felt my spirits lift. It was indeed a magnificent, extraordinary place that rose before me, at the far end of the ride, a soft grey stone house, with a wing on either side, and a flight of steps curving up to the front doors.

Before it, set in the centre of the sweeping, circular drive, was a huge fountain, and great urns flanked the pillars of the porch. The door stood open, and light from within streamed into the gathering dusk – indeed, every window was full of light, the shimmer of glass chandeliers mingling with the softer light of candles banked on stands. I saw a classical orangery, and, as we turned into the drive at last, caught a glimpse of lawns stretching away behind the house into the darkness, of high walls and lily ponds, pleached walks and more fountains, and a slope descending out of sight towards the gleam of the lake.

Then, we were stopped, and Lady Quincebridge was at the door and coming quickly down the steps to greet me and I was swept up from that moment into the splendour and brilliance of her world, as well as the warmth and sincerity of her welcome. When I stepped inside the house, I felt as if I were being enveloped in light and richness, and cocooned in the comforts and splendour of the Christmas setting.

The house was magnificent, with a great hall, and staircase rising up from it, dark wood panelling and old, polished furniture gleaming in the blaze of the log fires that burned in every room. The Christmas tree, decorated with baubles and painted fir cones, candles and ribbon, reached up almost to touch the high ceiling, the fireplaces and door

[108]

mantles were swathed with holly and the whole house smelled sweetly of woodsmoke, pungent fruits and green branches. I stood, dazzled by it all, but at once Lady Quincebridge was at my side, concerned and full of friendliness.

'Weston will show you up – your bag has already gone. Now do make yourself at home and familiar with everything, and wash and so forth, as you wish. You are looking tired, Mr Monmouth.'

She laid a hand lightly on my arm for a second, looking carefully into my face. 'There is something wrong,' she said in a low voice, 'I can see it, sense it, something has happened to you. Well, you are safe here, we will look after you. Now – there will be tea in the drawing room, when you come down. The place is full of children, you will hear them all about, but mainly at the top of the house, and at least they take their tea together in the nursery, you will not have to face the little monsters just now!'

I murmured my thanks and followed the man up the staircase and, when I glanced back, saw that she was watching me, her face sombre and clouded, yet her expression, as I had once before seen it, oddly distant too.

At the top of the stairs I came, with a start, face to face with Lady Quincebridge again – or, rather, with her portrait, a magnificent, full-length study. She was portrayed standing in a conservatory, beside a camellia in flower, the windows behind her open onto a vista of the park that stretched away into the distance, and she wore a violet-blue evening dress, with a cascading train – the colour seemed to vibrate as I looked at it.

The walls of the upper corridor were lined with beautiful pictures, more portraits, still-life studies of bowls of hothouse fruit, and blowsy, drooping roses, elegant black gun dogs, men on horseback, and small, exquisite chalk drawings of children, of a dancer, of a kitten, and again and again of Lady Quincebridge, sketches of her head, resting on her hand, or standing brushing her long hair forwards;

and then some landscapes of the house and gardens and park, formal and serene.

The man opened a door at the far end of the corridor, and I followed him into my room.

The curtains were drawn across the windows, and, when I glanced out, I saw that darkness had fallen so that I could get no sense even of the direction the room faced.

I turned and looked about me, at the fine furnishings, the wood, the canopied bed, the pleasing pictures – nothing was overpowering or intimidating to me, everything had been provided for my comfort and ease, and it struck me, perhaps fully for the first time, how generous and trusting it was of my hosts to invite a virtual stranger into their home at this season. I was grateful, and I resolved to repay their kindness by being as model a guest as I knew how.

The man had indicated that my bags would be unpacked for me, but I took out the gift I had brought for Lady Quincebridge, and, after washing, ventured back down the stairs. I had seen a pile of Christmas parcels arranged on a low stool beneath the tree, and I was setting my own down as unobtrusively as I could. It had not been easy to select something for people I scarcely knew, but I had found a small, delicately figured porcelain model of a pair of children dressed in the country clothes of the previous century and bought it because my instinct told me I had best choose what pleased my own eye and hope that my taste would be shared.

As I was setting it in place, I heard Lady Quincebridge behind me. 'Mr Monmouth – now do come into the drawing room and have tea. We are only family and a couple of friends just now – but we are a very large party for dinner, over forty, I'm afraid – it has become a tradition and we can't see any way of giving it up!'

I followed her towards the fireplace at the far end of the long room, where tea was set out among a group of sofas and chairs, and made my first acquaintance with the rest of the house party.

There were various sisters, and cousins, a married son and two daughters with their spouses, a great-aunt – I was confused by them, now, though later I came to separate and know them better. There were also a married couple and a bachelor friend – and Sir Lionel Quincebridge himself.

'It is extremely kind of you to welcome me here,' I said. 'I am a stranger to you, yet you invite me freely and openly. It would have been a bleak enough Christmas for me otherwise, I confess.'

He shook my hand. 'My wife has often made friends in this way, Mr Monmouth, and somehow her instinct is unerring.'

'And has her trust never been misplaced or betrayed?'

'Never – though, of course, she does not go about inviting people by the score, only now and again. I believe it is the Biblical imperative with her – to bring in guests from the highways and byways and welcome them to one's table!'

He was a handsome man, tall, with a leonine head of grey hair, and a slight stoop from the shoulders. His manner was welcoming and friendly without reserve, yet I detected a shrewdness and alertness in his eyes and in one or two of his questions that told me he would not be an easy man to deceive, and that he acted as a balance and temper to any impetuosity on the part of his wife.

I talked to him a good deal that evening, and over the course of the following days, and found him to be a man of wide learning and sound judgement, manifold interests and a great good humour. He was sociable, personable, amiable, yet I sensed that he had strength in reserve and a cutting edge, too, which he might employ to devastating effect. In short, he was a fine lawyer, who had reached the top of his profession with ease. The house and estate, he told me almost at once, had come to them through his wife's family – Lady Quincebridge was a woman of substantial means.

At dinner, a tremendous, glittering affair, I was seated halfway down the long table, next to a lawyer friend and neighbour, and one of the married Quincebridge daughters. From the latter, I learned about the neighbourhood – she and her young family lived only a short distance away, and she was a happy, easy companion. But it was the former, whose name was Geoffrey Ludgate, who drew me out skilfully on the subject of my travels. His particular interest, like mine, was in the far east, and most of all China, about which he was well informed, yet he appeared to want to hear everything I could tell him nonetheless and I realised how skilfully Lady Quincebridge had arranged her table and combined her guests.

At one point in the course of our conversation, I mentioned that several of my more adventurous journeys had followed the paths pioneered by Conrad Vane and described by him in his travel journals. At the mention of Vane's name, Ludgate paused, fork to mouth, and gave me a penetrating stare, and I noticed also that a silence had fallen briefly at the head of the table where Sir Lionel was sitting.

When the general talk resumed, I asked Ludgate quietly if he knew anything of Vane.

'Only what is – common knowledge,' he said guardedly, lifting his glass.

'And that is?'

He waved a hand. 'Oh, rumour, conjecture merely.'

'But of an unpleasant nature?'

'Somewhat.'

'So I have discovered. I have been delving into his life and past – I had thought of writing some sort of study of the man – of Vane, the traveller, the explorer, that is.'

'But?'

'I have been rather deterred. And other matters of keener personal interest have begun to preoccupy my attention.'

'That would seem to be as well. No good ever seems to have come to anyone from too close a contact with Vane and his affairs.'

'But the man is dead.'

'Indeed.'

'You have personal knowledge?'

'Oh no, no. As I said – there is rumour, I have heard tales. One remembers this and that.'

After which he changed the subject firmly and began to question me about my boyhood in Kenya, a country with which he told me his father had had connections, and the slight ruffle in the surface of the conversation was smoothed over again.

It was as enjoyable and impressive an evening as I had ever spent in my life, the food excellent, the setting resplendent, the atmosphere convivial and festive. Before dinner, we had been visited by a party of young carol singers, who had come in from the murky, dismal night to stand around the tree and entertain us, and the children of the house party, at least a dozen of them, had all, save for the infants, been allowed to join us. The light of their sweet faces, their bright eyes, their air of excitement and anticipation, had filled me with a tenderness and yearning I had never before known, and, looking at them, I longed for my own family, and to have a place in which I could belong, and those I could call my own and dear to me – such sentiments did the old words and sacred Christmas tunes stir within me.

So enjoyable was the time, and so thoroughly was I swept up into the company, and so overawed by the occasion, the setting, and my own presence in the house, that I was able to ignore any reminders that I was unwell; from time to time during dinner I had felt my skin burn, at others I shivered and longed to creep close to the fire. I drank little wine, and in all suffered a general feeling of malaise, but I was able to ignore it until the very end of the evening, when I rose to make my way to bed. There were only the resident family and two other house guests left and it was past midnight. As I stood up I experienced a violent giddiness, which caused me to stagger, and at the same moment, my skull felt as if it had been split open by an axe blow. I found myself seated again, with Sir Lionel gripping my arm, but I tried to make light of the incident pleading extreme tiredness, and in the end persuaded him that a calm night's sleep would restore me completely.

I was not confident that this would be so, however, and, alone in my room, gave way to a shivering fit and dosed myself with whisky before getting gratefully into my bed.

That night, I tossed, now as if I lay on burning coals, now on rivers of ice, and my sleep was broken and jagged by nightmares, full of fleeting, horrible images all jumbled together. Then, abruptly, I woke, and all was still, I half came to my senses, and as I did so saw that the fire that had been burning in the bedroom hearth when I retired was still glowing a little at its heart. My head ached, my mouth was dry, and there was a rawness in my chest, as if it were full of rusty filings that grated when I breathed.

And then, for a few, tantalising seconds, I remembered everything. I was a small child again, lying in bed in a room with a few lighted coals in the grate. I was ill, my head ached, my chest was painful as I breathed. And beside me, on a low chair drawn up close to the bed, sat – sat someone, whose face I had just seen in my dream, as clearly as if she had just been here.

But now she was gone, and I was no longer a child, safe in my familiar bed, being nursed and watched over, I was alone in a strange house, wretchedly unwell. I could have wept with frustration, and wanted to run back into the safe arms of my dream.

I turned on the lamp.

'James Monmouth, his, to remember Old Nan.'

I reached for the small black Prayer Book that lay on the table close by, and after contemplating the inscription for some time, which gave me a strange feeling of contentment I could not explain, I began to turn the pages, reading here and there at random, and realised that every now and again the words were so familiar that I had them by heart – though when and how I had learned them I did not recall. At last, though still feeling ill, I fell into a more peaceful sleep, and awoke, weak but in some measure restored, to the sound of the bells of Christmas morning.

Breakfast was brought to me, together with a message from Lady Quincebridge which enquired after my health and insisted that I need not venture down at all unless I felt quite fit. But, although weak, I thought that my fever seemed to have burned itself out during the night, and I determined that I could not miss the festivities of the day, or be a miserable guest. I managed to eat a little, and drank copious quantities of tea, after which I felt greatly restored.

I saw now that my room had a view of the park, which stretched away, beyond the formal lawns at the back of the house. It was a bright day, but a mist wreathed between the lower trunks of the avenues of trees, out of which rose the ghostly bodies of deer and cattle. But the sun was coming up and, as I watched, the mist began to dissolve and float away, and I could see the landscape in all its beauty, as it undulated towards a ha-ha, and rose gently on the other side. The lake I could just glimpse, steely in the early morning light, and as I looked a flight of duck flew over and skimmed down onto it.

Between the trees a broad path crossed the grass, with another, narrower, winding in a more leisurely fashion around the parameters, and I was anxious, if I felt strong enough, to walk there soon. For I had fallen in love with Pyre, the handsome house and its grounds; it was a good place, which seemed to have no sinister or hostile shades within or without, and I blessed my good fortune at meeting with Lady Quincebridge by such chance on the train to Alton. My fears, the strange and unnerving events of the past weeks, were fading from my mind; I did not feel that I must turn my head and look behind me everywhere I went, and no longer dwelt constantly, to the disturbance of my peace of mind, on the thought of whatever poor creatures, real or imagined, had followed and haunted me.

Just after ten, I went down. My head was still sore, my limbs aching, but I was sure I could manage to enjoy this Christmas day.

To my surprise, instead of lively excitement and bustle, I heard no sound save my own footsteps, the house was hushed and seemed quite deserted.

In the Hall, Weston met me, and told me that the party had gone to church.

'Lady Quincebridge was adamant you should not try and join them, sir, in view of your state of health. She particularly asked me to say that you should rest in beside the fire. They will be back by noon.'

'Thank you. Everyone is being very kind. I have nothing more than a touch of some ague – I shall be perfectly well again directly.'

'There is a good fire in the morning room then, sir, and you will find *old* Mr Quincebridge there.'

He went cheerfully away.

For a little while, I stood, looking at the tree, enjoying its spread and stature, and the brightness of its decorations. All was peaceful and serene, and I felt as secure and safe as I believe a man may ever feel. The house, or at least this part of it, might be quiet, and I almost alone, and yet I felt somehow enfolded and protected by an atmosphere that was wholly benign, partly because of the influence of the season of Christmas itself, but more, because love and warmth, generosity and openness, welcome and friendship, were settled there and I felt had long been so, so that they were part of the very fabric of the place, in the bricks and stone and panelling and furnishings, in the very air itself.

I turned and went across the hall to the morning room. It was light, airy, handsome, with cream-painted shutters folded back from the tall windows that overlooked a rose garden at the side of the house, and pale, sea-green walls on which hung rows of drawings and pastels. A huge brass bowl of holly stood on a central table, and the fire crackled with freshly laid sticks and logs.

And beside the fire, settled so deep in a wing chair that at first I did not see he was there at all, was the gentleman I took to be *old* Mr Quincebridge.

He appeared to be asleep. He was enfolded in a large tartan blanket which was pulled up almost to his chin, and his eyes were closed. I went quietly into the room, and then paused, unwilling to disturb him, and remained looking out of the window, at the bare, pruned twigs of the rose bushes. The clock ticked softly, the fire sputtered every so often, but otherwise all was silent. I rather envied him his peaceful situation. He had not appeared either at tea or dinner on Christmas Eve and I wondered if he lived at Pyre or had been brought over only this morning.

'Take a seat, my dear sir, take a seat.'

His eyes were now huge and alert, gleaming from out of the parchment-coloured skull. His long legs stuck out from beneath the rug, and, together with his stick-like arms and etiolated neck, they gave him the appearance of a grasshopper folded up into the chair. He had two or three small tufts of white hair sprouting up like thistledown on a dandelion clock, enormous ears and taut, stretched skin.

I went to shake the hand he extended to me. It was like shaking a bunch of long, thin bones. He was colourless, and almost transparent, and desiccated, but in the bright eyes

and the raised blue veins at his neck and temple and wrist I
saw that the thread of life still beat steadily.

'Take a seat, sir.'

I did so, pulling the chair opposite to him closer to the
fire. His voice was surprisingly strong, his eyes steady on
my face.

'It is Christmas Day,' he said.

'It is indeed – may I wish you the best compliments of
the season? I am told that the rest of the party are at church
and I feel I should have been with them, but I had a touch
of chill last night and Lady Quincebridge insisted I should
remain by the fire.'

'You are not a neighbour. *I* have never seen you.'

'No, sir, I am a mere acquaintance – though I would
hope to be able to call myself a friend, as I have been
offered the hand of friendship so readily.'

'This is my son's house. Lionel. He is my only son,
though I had others.' He spoke matter-of-factly, as though
he were too old, and long past whatever sadness there
might once have been.

'It is a fine house. I admire it very much.'

He did not reply, and I saw that his eyes were closed
again. He seemed to have gone instantly to sleep, in the
way only the very old and the very young do, in the midst of
a sentence or a stream of thought. I leaned back, still feeling that my illness, whatever it might be, was hovering in
the wings just out of sight, and likely to return viciously at
any moment. But it was soothing to sit here, without any
disturbance or anxiety, in the old man's company. A tray of
coffee was brought and I waited, wondering what to do,
but, in the end, poured my own, as quietly as I could. I was
drinking it, and looking at a delicate drawing of a girl in a
pony-cart, when he woke again as abruptly as he had slept.

'Monmouth,' said old Mr Quincebridge. 'Monmouth. I
knew a Monmouth.'

I leaned forwards.

'Where? Did I? I wonder. Monmouth.'

'If you were to remember anything, I should like to hear it. I . . .'

'Yes, yes. I would be obliged if you would pour me a cup of tea.'

'It is coffee. Shall I ring for tea?'

'No, no, no.' He shuffled a little, rummaged his legs about.

'If there is anything . . .'

'It is Christmas Day,' he said again.

I was desperate for him to return to the subject of my name.

'I am particularly anxious to discover anything about my family,' I said. 'I know nothing – I was sent to Africa, to a guardian at the age of five, I presume after the death of my parents, and I have only recently returned from many years – all my adult life – lived abroad, but I am certain there must be those who remember – who can give me some clue as to my parentage, know the place from which I came.'

'All dead,' he said, slipping down into the folds of his rug again.

'Dead?' How could he know? What did he mean?

'I am ninety-four.' His eyes were closing again. He muttered my name in a vague, puzzled way once or twice, and then slept.

I sat on opposite to him, my head aching again, and with a burning soreness behind my eyes, thinking, thinking, turning over what he had said in my mind. He was ninety-four. Sir Lionel had been at Alton, and I was aware that English families tended to keep to tradition in such matters. If old Mr Quincebridge had been at the school, surely he would have been almost a contemporary of Vane? And therefore also of George Edward Pallantire Monmouth of Kittiscar.

I wanted to shake him roughly to wake him, question him, force him to remember. But, when I looked at him again, I saw a fragile, old, old man, only clinging on to this world, this life, by a frail skein, already half-adrift, like a kite up in the clouds of some other future. I could no more have broken into his sleep than into that of a baby. But I determined that later, after the festivities of the day were over, I would talk to him again, probe gently, try and tease awake some memory, some scrap for me to grasp.

In the peace and quietness of that calm room, I too closed my eyes and slept a little, like another old, tired man, and woke with some embarrassment as Lady Quincebridge came in to find us, followed by the rest of the party; and so we began to celebrate Christmas, I doing my best to conceal my increasing fever and sickness, and enjoy what I could of the feasting and entertainment, the happy company.

I succeeded until evening, when I collapsed again, this time more seriously. A doctor was sent for, and I was helped by two of the servants to my bed, and for many days I was wretchedly ill, tossing with a fever, and blinding headache, slipping down and down into the dark, swirling waters of delirium time and time again, unsure even who or where I was. I was attended to and nursed with great devotion and, weak and wretched as I was, could only accept gratefully.

CHAPTER ELEVEN

The last time I remembered being in this room, a very old man had been huddled in a chair beside the fire.

Now, I was that old man, or felt like one, and I sat there, the rug tucked warmly about my legs. But the room was not cold, and a little thin sunshine even shone in through the windows. I could see trails of white cloud stretched across a pale, watery sky.

'Is there anything you would like? You have only to ask me.'

Lady Quincebridge sat nearby, half turned to me, half to look out of the window, a piece of embroidery resting on her lap.

I had no idea how long I had slept – I had been sleeping on and off for days, my sense of time had become blurred. But I remembered coming down the stairs that morning, helped by Weston, for the first time since I had been taken ill on Christmas Day. Even that small effort had exhausted me, but the doctor who had been attending me had insisted that I was ready to make the first move out of the sick room. 'Illness can become a habit, and feed upon itself,' he had said. 'You are past the worst and embarked on the road to recovery. We shall have you take it step by step.'

It was extremely pleasant, I thought, to sit here in this quiet room again, weak, light-headed, but knowing that from now I would gradually become stronger.

Lady Quincebridge smiled. 'You are looking better. You are with us again.'

'Yes.' She was right, for I had been wandering in some confused, shadowy limbo of illness and fever, out of touch with the reality of my surroundings.

'It seems that I have been absent for some time,' I said.

'Over two weeks. Christmas is long past.'

'Christmas.' I scarcely remembered it. But the old man who had muttered my own name was vividly before my eyes and I wanted to ask her about him – I presumed he was Sir Lionel's father. I wanted to ask if it would be possible to talk to him again, and I realised that my interest in things was returning, for until now I could not have cared a straw for myself, my past, my name, anything that had been so preoccupying me.

But first, looking at her, I said, 'When we met on the train that dark afternoon, you told me that you were anxious for my safety, that you had had some kind of premonition.'

'Indeed yes.'

'But how? Why?'

'I do not know where these things come from, Mr Monmouth, I have never understood, never enquired. I have learned to trust them. Ever since I was a child, I have been sometimes subject to overwhelmingly powerful intuitions. I have been with a person, and known, for example, that they were soon to die – that is the worst of all. It is as though there is a clear voice that speaks in my head, and, at the same time, a shadow falls over me – and over them. I grow cold, I am afraid. Or else it is that I am urgently aware of some danger. I see dark shapes, formless but quite clear – it is rare nowadays. But I have been right so often, I have learned to listen, and to respect them. When I met you that day, I had almost forgotten these experiences, it had not happened to me for several years. But I knew – you were in some danger – you were . . .'

'To die?'

'No. No, it was not that. But I felt afraid – and there was something – evil, harmful . . . some dark and dreadful thing – I could not tell what.'

For a while I was silent, gradually, slowly, because of my own weakness, trying to trace back to my arrival in London and remember all of the things I had seen or sensed, to recall the warnings I had received from Beamish, Votable, Dancer, as well as everything I had learned at Alton, about Conrad Vane.

At last I looked up. Her eyes were on my face. I began to talk.

Outside the windows, the clouds massed together and the sun went behind them, the morning room grew darker. Rain spattered lightly on the windows.

Lady Quincebridge listened without interrupting me, sewing the petals of some pale blue flower on her embroidery. The fire sank down, but she did not get up to attend to it.

From the hall, the clock struck twelve.

I finished my story with the inscription in the Prayer Book, and told her what slight but definite flickers of memory it woke deep within me, whenever I read or even so much as thought about it.

I closed my eyes, suddenly giddy and exhausted again by the effort of talking and concentrating my mind for so long. I heard Lady Quincebridge move out of the room and, after a few moments, return with Weston. A tray was set down beside me.

'Here is a little brandy and water – it will revive you.'

When I leaned forward to take it, my hand trembled, and she hastened over to lift the glass for me. But, after sipping it, I felt better and able to talk a little again.

[123]

'I had begun to feel that everywhere I went was a haunted place, and to wonder why I had such ill luck. I had never experienced these things in other countries – why was it in England that I felt observed, followed?'

'Perhaps – it has nothing to do with the places themselves – or not altogether,' she said.

'No. I have thought of that – that it is I who am haunted – *I* who disturb these ghosts by my presence, no matter where I am, *I* who am being pursued. The things I have seen and heard and sensed have not been accidental, I am sure of it. They are deliberate – meant.'

'Oh yes.'

'You believe me? You have not said that you think me mistaken? Or mad?'

'No, and I also think that your illness has been inevitable – that you have been under such a great strain and bearing it quite alone – you were bound to succumb to something, and perhaps it has been a good thing, it has given you pause, taken you away from this mad pursuit, this quest that had come to obsess you.'

'I am only relieved that I was able to be here at Pyre, despite the trouble it has caused to your household, and the interruption to your lives.'

'Perhaps that, too, was inevitable, from the moment of our meeting. When you are recovered fully, you will be very much further away from all that has happened since your arrival in England. You will be able to look to your future more clearly.'

'My future,' I said blankly. I had no idea what that might be. Everything I had been planning, and the book I meant to write about Conrad Vane, seemed to be part of another life altogether. I wondered if any of it would ever interest me again, my mental powers seemed so debilitated. But if not that, then what? What purpose had I? I had none, and could not imagine what the future she spoke of might possibly be.

'You will stay here at Pyre until you are completely well. Lionel and I are quite decided about that.'

I thanked her, as it seemed I had been doing every day of my illness, very conscious that I could do nothing more.

'And then will be time enough for you to look ahead. You have reached a cross-roads – a crisis in your life. You cannot rush forwards and risk taking the wrong path.'

I sipped the last of my brandy. I was beginning to feel drowsy again.

'This is a good place,' I said. 'I have no fears – the shadows are all dispersed. Nothing touches me here.'

'I am profoundly glad of it.'

As I drifted off to sleep, I remembered the old man and would have asked her about him now, stressed how much I wanted to see him again, to find out what he knew of the name Monmouth, but I was too tired to speak, and the thoughts became muddled up with others. I would do it later, I told myself.

Monmouth, he had muttered. I heard his feeble, creaking old voice now. Monmouth.

I slept.

At his invitation, I took to spending the evenings in Sir Lionel's study, a shabby, comfortable room at the back of the house, booklined, with deep armchairs, and the old black labrador Fenny stretched out on the hearthrug. Here, as we drank a glass of whisky, our talk ranged over my travels and the present situation of those countries I had come to know so well, and I learned from him a great deal which had previously been unclear to me, of the ways of English life, and its politics and constitution as well as its society, of how the country worked, and of Sir Lionel's particular branch of the criminal law. He talked of his own boyhood, much of which had been spent happily in Scotland – he was an Edinburgh man by birth, and, I sensed, still hankered after it – of his time in South Africa and France as a soldier, of men he had known, landscapes he loved, and of his family, too. The longer I spent in his company, the more I liked and admired him. He seemed to me a man of sound and shrewd judgement, courage and a generous and contented heart.

It was he who suggested that I should begin making a formal plan of work.

'Stay here with us for another week or two,' he said one night, as we sat beside the flickering fire. Outside, the wind was tearing at the trees of the park, and roaring across towards the house, to beat at the windows, but in here all was safe and snug, the lamps casting deep pools on the desk and books, and on Sir Lionel's handsome features, as he sat, legs outstretched, sucking at his pipe.

'You are better, but your strength has been greatly depleted, you have been under strain and you are not yet up to coping with winter days and nights, alone in London in an empty house. Why not get into some routine of work here? I have always found that best, it concentrates the mind and settles one, provides a framework for thought.'

'Yes. I confess I have done little of it, I have been my own master and fancy free – not to mention a nomad – for so long.'

'Divide up your life and your travels, take each part separately – Africa and your boyhood there, then China and the far east – and South America – go back over the journeys in your mind, retrace your steps, remember everything you can – you have interested me as you have talked these past nights, you have an excellent recall, and a good turn of phrase, your observations are sharp. You must not let it all go to waste.'

And so I began, on the following morning. A small table was set for me in the library, a grand but, I sensed, little-used room; when Sir Lionel wanted books he either took them off to his own study, or sat with Lady Quincebridge.

The library felt slightly cold, and bleak; it faced north, and got little sun. But a fire was lit for me and, although it smoked a bit and would not burn up, I settled happily enough in a window bay, before a fresh sheaf of paper. I took down the world atlas at first and sat looking through it, setting down places and dates, going over routes and listing them. He was right: as I did so, the countries in all their individual detail and atmosphere came vividly back to me, I remembered faces, buildings, even talk, the play of light on land and water, smells. My past was not lost to me, and, in retrieving it, I began to recover my youth and some of the sense of my own identity which I had lost since arriving in England.

I worked with growing excitement and enthusiasm for several hours, and, when at last my brain was too fagged for me to continue, sat on quietly, satisfied that I was doing the right thing and had found the beginning of the path to the future.

Once or twice, as I went over the journeys I had undertaken and remembered why I had ventured to this or that remote and obscure place, the name of Conrad Vane came to my mind, but I turned away from it, for I was determined not to be misled in that direction again – though it still puzzled me that the man I had believed in and admired by every account had such another, dark side to his character. I wanted to forget the influence he had had over me, and was ashamed to have made such a grave error, albeit innocently, for so long.

But, now, I was myself, James Monmouth, these had been my journeys, and the story I intended to tell was mine alone.

For the next few days I worked peacefully and steadily in this way every morning, going to the library immediately after breakfast, as soon as Sir Lionel went off to London and his chambers, and, as he had predicted, the routine began to settle and steady me, so that my strength grew, my head was clear, and I began to feel a new confidence in myself. The material in the pages before me was at first set down almost at random, simply as it came into my head, but I soon began to give it a shape, and to discipline my thoughts and memories to come to order. It seemed to me that I would be able to write two books, the one about my boyhood and upbringing in Africa and India, and the second, entirely about my time in the east.

The weather was dull and often wet – we were having a mild winter, but I walked every day in the park, enjoying its broad vistas, and the elegant landscape, and, as I felt stronger, extended the time I spent outside and went beyond the grounds of Pyre, into the lanes and scattered small villages of the surrounding countryside. Many a time I returned by way of the River Thames which flowed, broad and strong, only a mile or two from the house. Usually the dog Fenny would accompany me, and chase a stick, rather sedately, for she was elderly now and often had to be nudged away from the fireside. Otherwise, I saw almost no one.

I had been at work for a week when several friends and neighbours came to dine, and in the course of the general conversation one, a legal colleague of Sir Lionel's, happened to mention a journey he had taken north the previous autumn.

'I went with Mortensen,' he was saying to Sir Lionel, 'and he's a man to venture off into the bush. It was far from my usual beat but I must admit that we had a superb day's shooting in glorious country – ' He turned to me. 'You have been a traveller, Mr Monmouth,' he said, 'and I daresay have seen many fine sights but I defy you or anyone to paint to me a grander prospect than the countryside spread out below Rook's Crag, looking over to Kittiscar.'

My fork clattered onto my plate.

'*Kittiscar!*'

Lady Quincebridge put her hand on my arm. They were all four of them staring at me in alarm.

'Dear God, man, what have I said?' he asked. 'You are ashen.'

'Kittiscar,' I choked at last. 'You said Kittiscar.'

'I did.'

'Then I beg you to tell me about it – to describe it – show me the place on a map – tell me anything . . .' I almost got to my feet then. 'I must know!'

CHAPTER TWELVE

'It is,' he said, 'the most wild and beautiful part of the country.' He nodded across to Sir Lionel. 'You would not rate it much below your beloved Highlands for grandeur.'

We were seated around the table after the ladies had retired, and the man who had spoken was the lean, sharp-featured lawyer, Crawford Maythorn.

'It is rugged fell country, with rounded hills and gentle slopes, shelving down to small villages, mostly set beside the fast-flowing streams that run all over those parts. It's sheep country – hardy little things, scattered about the hillsides. There are no large towns for many miles – not many people either, for such great expanses and those there are huddle together and see precious few strangers – except in high summer, when the walking parties are out. Sheep and grouse – eagles, too, and buzzards occasionally, up on the crags.' He smoked his pipe appreciatively. 'I tell you, to sit up there and watch the shadows chasing one another over the open hills, to see the sunlight catching on clusters of slate roofs far below, and hear nothing but the wind keening and the bleating of the sheep – ' He shook his head.

I listened, seated tense and straight in my chair. He had described a countryside I knew, as he spoke I felt sure that it was familiar, and I had been there, seen these things, my whole being responded to his words. He had not told me about Kittiscar itself, but now he turned to me.

'I have looked across at it,' he said, 'but I do not usually venture as far off the beaten track. Just once, though, I did go; it was two or three years ago. I am afraid there is precious little I can tell you. Kittiscar is very small, a hamlet, no more, with the usual grey stone cottages – a chapel. The Inn is at Rook's Crag, a mile to the east.'

'There is a Hall, I believe.'

'Yes. I remember seeing some sign or gatepost, but nothing of the place itself. We got half lost up there one afternoon – it can be pretty bleak and forbidding in fading light and bad weather. But thankfully we scrambled down and managed to find the road again, and that led us to Raw Mucklerby.' He grunted in amusement. 'Now there I fancy you would find out anything you wanted to know about anyone else's business – history, biography, news, gossip. It seemed to be a popular stop for sportsmen such as ourselves, but most of all the meeting place for the locals from miles around. I'm quite sorry I shan't be up there this year.' He glanced across the table. 'I am promised to the Cairngorms with Quincebridge's party I think.' Sir Lionel confirmed it, and the talk then turned to matters of sport. After another ten minutes or so, I made my excuses, which, as I was still convalescent, were readily accepted, and went to bed.

The evening's conversation had disturbed me profoundly and I wanted to retreat into the cocoon of my illness, and of being protected and sheltered here in this house, for I was afraid now of what I would face when I ventured out of it. The description of the countryside by Kittiscar had awakened memories, and perhaps if I had delved more thoroughly into them I might have teased them to the surface, but instead I turned away from them deliberately, for I knew the frustration of trying to bring them to my consciousness. They would swirl and drift about, I would half-glimpse them, only to lose them again, as I had lost my own reflection through the mist in the mirror at Alton.

I had heard something, but not enough. Well, I would let it alone, I would set myself to the task in hand, write about the past I was sure of, the places I could vividly recall, and let the other go.

Nevertheless, the following morning, I took down the Atlas of Great Britain rather than of some other, far country, set it before me on the library table, and traced the pale brown spine of hills that ran north, following the names of Thwaites and Becks, Garths and Tarns, across to the most northerly hills. And then, veering a little west, I found those places I had heard of the previous night. Ashlaby. Bleet. Mucklerby. Raw Mucklerby. Rook's Crag. Kittiscar. And stared at them until the letters danced together on the page before my eyes.

Two days later, I received a note.

My dear Monmouth,

By chance, I have had to make contact with Mortensen, my shooting companion on the trip to the north last year, and I mentioned to him your possible connection with the area. He knows it a little better than I and he tells me that Kittiscar Hall is lived in by a woman. She is elderly and alone apart from the usual house staff. Her name is Miss Monmouth. Though he knows nothing more and has not been to the house, or ever seen her to his knowledge, I felt certain, in view of her name and of what you told me, that this information would be of some interest to you.

  Sincerely
  Crawford Maythorn

Now, I thought, it is pursuing me. It is I who have tried to turn my back and am fleeing. I crushed the letter up in my hand, and threw it into the fire.

'You are troubled about something,' Lady Quincebridge said. We were in her own small sitting room on the first floor of the house. Tea was over, the empty cups and plates beside us. The curtains were drawn. 'You have been so much more settled and easy, your work has begun to absorb you, and you have gradually extended your walks so that I have had high hopes of your complete recovery very soon.'

'Yes.'

'It is this business about Kittiscar. If I had known what Maythorn was to say, how the whole subject would arise . . .'

'Yet only a week ago I was the one desperate – hungry – for any crumb of information. I have longed to know my past – my history – if only to take my mind off all thoughts of Conrad Vane and his devilries. I have the Prayer Book beside me on the bedside chest. I look at it every night before sleep. Yet now I have something real within my grasp . . .'

'You are afraid?'

'Is it that? But why? What have I to fear?'

'You will not know unless . . .'

'Unless I go there. Discover for myself. You are right, of course.'

I bent forwards to stroke the cat, Missy, who sat on the rug, squinting into the fire.

'The truth is,' I said miserably, 'I have become comfortable here, and perhaps I have taken advantage of your kindness. I came for Christmas, a day or two at most. I have been here nigh on a month.'

'Because you needed us. You were friendless, homeless, and without roots in this country which was new and strange to you. And then you were ill. How could we have sent you away in such a state?' She smiled. 'Besides you have been good company to two old sticks. We rattle about here, we are set in our own ways, and little comforts, but at the very least we can share them when it pleases us.'

'Nevertheless . . .'

'Wait a little longer – until the next turn of the year, when there is a sign of spring. It will not be long. But you would have a hard journey and a cold time of it so far north at the back end of January. Go to London, if you are rest-less now, and visit us again for a few days before you set off. You will be welcome here at any time. Wait a few weeks yet.'

I agreed thankfully, and also said that I would stay at Pyre a few more days, until my work was well under way, and I felt entirely well – for I still tired wretchedly at the end of a walk and fell asleep in my chair, if I was not careful, after dinner.

We played a game of piquet in a pleasantly quarrelsome way then, until the car brought Sir Lionel home from the railway station, and his day in London.

When I went to my desk in the library the following morn-ing, I intended to add several more pages to my African journal. I had made a good beginning, I thought, the mem-ories had come flooding back, and it was a great pleasure and satisfaction to me to be able to recall my Guardian, our neighbours, the servants I had come to know so well, the places in which I had spent my boyhood, and which I had loved.

But, when I set pen to paper, it was not of outdoor days in Northern Kenya that I began to write. As though I were taken over by a force quite outside myself, I began a letter.

Dear Miss Monmouth,
My name, as you will see below, is your name. I have in my possession a Prayer Book given to me as a

child, and inscribed, as from Kittiscar Hall. Whether we are related, I do not know, but it seems most likely. I have lately returned from many years, since childhood, spent abroad, at first in the care of a guardian and after his death, some twenty years ago, alone. I am now returned to England, which I left at the age of five, and at present with friends, where any communication would reach me. My London lodgings are at Number 7, Prickett's Green, Chelsea, S.W.

I intend to make the journey north to Kittiscar in the early spring. What you know of me, if anything at all, I would very much wish to hear, and to have information about any other members of the family, living and dead.

Sincerely
James Monmouth

Having written the letter, I put the subject from my mind and turned back to Africa.

The weather changed, as January went out; it became mild again with fitful sunshine. A couple of days after I had written the letter to Miss Monmouth of Kittiscar, I took the dog Fenny and set off from the house, in the early afternoon. We walked at leisure between the graceful trees of the park, seeing the small deer ahead in the near distance, but they grazed on safely, unperturbed by the amiable old dog. I had begun to make my plans to return to London after the coming weekend. I was feeling more or less fit now, apart from tiredness at the end of each day, and needed to find a somewhat more extensive library of books about my subject. I also thought that I might visit Theodore Beamish's curious little shop again and dig about for some rare items there.

We came down the slope and the lake lay before us, its gunmetal surface still and smooth, reflecting the winter sun. All around me, the banks were white with clumps of snowdrops, heads bent upon their delicate stems, and pale gold aconites nestled beneath the trees. I had come to identify and enjoy these simple English flowers, they moved me, and pleased my eye more than anything vivid and exotic had ever done, and standing here now, as Fenny snuffled among the mulch and fallen twigs, after some old scent, I resolved that I would one day make a garden, and that it would be full of these delightful half-wild flowers, and of daffodils, of which I had heard so much from Lady Quincebridge.

'You must be sure to return for a day or so at the beginning of March,' she had said, 'the daffodils stretch right across the park and sweep down to the lake – Pyre is quite famous for them.'

But, for the moment, the snowdrops were enough for me, and I rested my back against one of the beeches, to drink in the sight of them and try to imprint it upon my memory.

Then I saw him. He had come a little way out from between the trees on the far side of the lake, and was standing there, apparently looking down at the water. The boy. His head was bare, he wore the same torn, white shirt, and grey trousers. His face was as pale as ever, deathly pale. I could see it quite clearly. He did not move away.

My heart was bursting within my chest. This was no ghost, this was a real, living boy; if I went to him now I would be able to touch him, speak to him, question him, there was nothing shadowy or insubstantial about him. So he had followed me here to Pyre, found me out in some way.

And then he looked up, deliberately, knowing full well that I was there, and we were face to face across the expanse of the lake. His expression was as it had been each time I had seen him, distant, anxious, pleading, and it distressed me beyond bearing. I could not move. I was petrified in time and place standing there in the silence. I saw that the dog's hackles had risen and that she was alert and quivering slightly, staring in the boy's direction.

The sun slipped behind a cloud and a slight breeze roughened the water and stirred the heads of the snowdrops.

'Who are you?' I called out then. 'Who are you and what do you want of me? Why have you come to me again?' He stood motionless and silent, staring, staring, and his look sent a chill of fear, and desperation through me. I began to move. 'Wait,' I shouted. 'Wait there.'

But he did not. He turned away slowly, sadly, his head bent. He was further away than I had thought, and I had to get over the rough grass and then halfway round the lake. The path dipped down as it turned. I followed it, half-running, the dog at my heels.

When I came up the rise again, the path ahead, and the places between the trees, the whole of the park that stretched away ahead, were empty. The boy had gone.

The dog Fenny ran round in circles, sniffing first at the ground, then, nose up, into the air, before she came back to me, whimpering a little.

After a while, I turned back, picking up a couple of sticks to throw, encouraging her to follow me. But it was some time before she would give up, and leave the spot beside the lake, where the boy had been. I did not want to speak about what had happened and I did not have to. Apart from the servants, in their own part of the house, Pyre was empty. Lady Quincebridge had gone up to London to join her husband for a dinner and it would be the early hours of the next morning before the car brought them back.

When I got in, I went to the library and tried to concentrate on my work, but the boy remained in my mind; his pale face and ragged form, his air of desperate pleading came before my eyes, so that after only a short time I gave up and sat brooding about him, addressing him in my thoughts. Who are you? Where do you come from? What are you asking of me?

But I knew who he was, I had known since I had been to Alton.

A fine rain was veiling the garden, the air was silver-grey, and I stood at the window for a while, looking mournfully out, half-expecting, even half-hoping, to see him again. He did not frighten me, whoever, whatever he was; I was puzzled by him, he challenged my sense of reality, made me question everything I saw around me. Above all, I did not understand how he could be apparently so solid, so *there*, if he was not. I knew that Viola Quincebridge, with her second sight, was aware of things unseen, of evil, danger and threats, and knew that she would at once pick up my disturbance of mood, and make me talk of the boy. I had felt immune from any strangeness here; until now, Pyre had been a wholly open and untroubled house. Now, it was not.

I went to sleep in my room for a couple of hours that afternoon, my head aching and my limbs heavy, as though some of the illness still hung about me and was dragging me down again. But I awoke somewhat refreshed and, after a quiet dinner, asked for the fire to be made up again in the library, and settled down at my desk.

At first, I worked well, and became deeply immersed in a particular account of a journey I had made with my Guardian into the tribal heartland of Kenya, when I was fourteen or so, a journey which had excited me and first awoken in me the desire to explore, to travel far into remote and primitive places. It had been an extraordinary time, the people friendly, welcoming and yet wholly alien, the country quite beautiful, most especially at dawn which, if I closed my eyes, I could see vividly before me, and hear the cries of the animals from the bush and the calls of the wild birds.

I wrote until my wrist ached and I was forced to set down my pen.

The fire, which never drew well in this chimney, was sluggish, black and smoking unpleasantly again, but the chill I felt around me had to do with more than that. The temperature was low and the air felt clammy, damp and stale. And, with the change of air, I felt something else, a presence in the room. I was being watched with hating, hostile eyes. I sat terrified, as I had been that night in the great library at Alton. Here, there was no gallery, and no possibility of anything being hidden behind the lines of bookcases, here I could look around the room and see everything, books on the walls, table, chairs, oak panelling, stone fireplace, the portrait of some jowly, beady-eyed ancestor with whip and stock that reared above it – the only unattractive picture in the house, and somehow, I had come to think, fittingly placed in this cold, hostile room.

I had not felt fear like this for weeks; indeed, I had never felt it at any time in this house, but now it came, and I was consumed by it, I wanted to cry out, my hands were wet, the hairs bristled upon my neck, my breathing was fast and shallow in my chest. Something was about to happen, something was here, evil and hatred, decay and cruelty were here and directed at me, and I could not escape.

I stood suddenly, knocking over my chair. I was seen. The eyes of the portrait bored into me, but it was not those eyes, hard and cold as they were, from whose stare I recoiled, it was from the gaze of someone I could not see.

'Who are you?' I whispered, my own voice choking in my throat. 'What do you want of me?'

The smoke from the fire belched out softly, I smelled it, sulphurous on the dank air, which now seemed like air not inside any room of a house, but rather the air of some dungeon or vault below ground.

I wanted to stumble out of the door and call for Weston, ask for a fire in the bright cheerfulness of the morning room, engage the man in a conversation just for the sake of his company, but I could neither move nor speak, it was as though I had been gripped by complete paralysis of the will and body, taken by an unseen, unknown presence and force. But it was not silent. I realised that now. For now, I heard the soft, regular sighing breathing; it seemed to be exuded by the walls at the fireplace end of the room. I stared and stared there, as if I could will whatever it was to materialise, but saw nothing, only heard, and was unable even to lift my hands to block out the sound, bound tight by invisible cords, and quite helpless.

I did not faint or cry out, I did nothing except close my eyes and wait, completely possessed by fear and by the presence in the room. In the end, it simply left. I was loosened from my bonds, I stumbled forwards to a chair, and sat, as the chill lifted, and a small spark of brightness flickered in the fire, and the only other sound was the gentle drumming of the rain on the roof and rolling down the gutters outside the window. The breathing simply stopped, the air lightened somehow. Even the old hunting squire was now merely solemn-faced and dull rather than malign of expression.

At last, I looked at my watch. I had set down my pen at a couple of minutes before ten. Hours had passed.

Then, the clock gathered itself, and struck, ten times.

I heard the opening of a door, footsteps, a knock, and Weston came in with the tray of whisky, and the usual plate of sandwiches. It was all I could do not to break down and weep with relief at the sight of him.

That night, I heard the sound of crying again, the same anguished sobbing I had first heard behind the locked door at Alton. It was in the room beyond my own, and it woke me. I lay listening to it without surprise, but rather, with a curious calm, for although it was as real to my ears as any earthly sound could be, I knew that what I heard was unearthly, and that, if I rose and went out to try and trace it, I would fail. I do not think I felt any fear then, only bewilderment and a determination first to try and understand it – for my common sense told me that it was not possible to lie here and listen to a sobbing that was quite clear, quite definite, and yet which was unreal and came from no living human source. I was being assailed on all sides and in all my senses, seeing, hearing, feeling things around me that were not there – yet *there*, truly, vividly there to me when they presented themselves.

I could not remain here – or, indeed, anywhere now – or rest, until I had followed my instincts and attended to these things, whatever they were. I had tried to ignore them, going from one place to another, and been pursued, and I was certain now that wherever I fled they would follow me and find me out.

In the past, if I had ever been lost in some remote place, and without any normal means of discovering in which direction I should go, I had quickly learned that it was best to obey my instincts and inner promptings, and to go the way I sensed, though without any external evidence, was right.

Now I was sure that I must act in the same way. For some reason that was quite unclear, I knew I must go to Kittiscar, indeed was being urged to go. I did not know why I felt strongly that what was happening to me, these hauntings, if such they were, had ultimately to do with that place and my past in it, but as I lay in the darkness of my room at Pyre, listening to the sound of the boy's desperate sobbing, I felt better, stronger and more confident, as well as calmer for having made that decision. And it was not a difficult one, I wanted to go, I had an inner conviction that I would find my own past at Kittiscar, that I had once belonged there, and perhaps did so still.

I fell into a doze, and gradually the sobbing faded and

the room was quiet again, save for the sound of rain on the windowpanes, a sound I had grown to love, partly because it was so different from the rain I had been used to abroad, rain that came in torrents, beating down madly upon frail buildings, gushing in fresh rivers outside, for days, weeks on end, and then, abruptly, ceased and came no more for months. But, as I drifted into sleep, I knew also that the soft rain here was a familiar, comforting sound from long ago, another echo of my childhood.

Two days later, I returned to Prickett's Green. Lady Quincebridge had not tried to prevent it, knowing, though she had said little, that something had happened to disturb my quietude the day she had gone up to London. But I had welcomed her insistence that I return to Pyre whenever I wished, at however short notice, and I was sure, as I looked back fondly at the house from the end of the long avenue, that I would do so, for I had become attached to it, and been in many ways protected and strengthened there, sheltered by the walls of the house and the affection of those good people.

I hoped to find a letter from Miss Monmouth of Kittiscar awaiting me, but there was none; I had no communication from anyone, but found only the empty-seeming rooms overlooking the wintry sky, the bare trees, and dark flowing river, and the footsteps of the lugubrious Threadgold on the stairs. I missed Pyre that night, the rooms, the warmth, the company. I went out for my supper, and sat in silence, reading a newspaper in the coffee house until very late, before going back to organise a few belongings, and make some brief arrangements.

It was early on a bright, spring-like morning that I set off again, for another railway station, and a train that was to take me on the long journey north, to Kittiscar.

CHAPTER THIRTEEN

I had taken books and journals to read in plenty and bought the daily newspapers at King's Cross, but I scarcely glanced at them, I was so absorbed in watching the countryside of England from out the carriage window, noting with fascination every change of scenery, from plain to hill to river valley, open farmland to black industrial chimneyscape. It interested and pleased me as well as any exotic landscape of my past travels.

As we journeyed further north, the weather began to change too; the sky, at first clear and mild, grew stormy, and I saw trees bending and tossing in the wind. Rain came, lashing the train windows, streams were rushing in angry spate down hillsides. But then we were out of it, and the clouds shifted again; I saw snow on the tops of the far hills.

I had consulted maps and guide books and found that a branch line would take me direct to the station at Raw Mucklerby, from High Beck Halt, though it seemed possible that I might have to wait some little time for a connection – the timetable was unclear. I meant to put up at the Inn which Sir Lionel's friend had spoken of, and set out to Kittiscar on the following morning.

The light began to fade for the last hour of the journey, and there were flurries of hard, stinging snow on the wind. But I was still exhilarated by the views, the grand, wild, open scenery of bare hills and moors, with greystone walls and small flinty villages and isolated farmhouses huddled into the lee of the slopes. There were sheep and, here and there, the sight of a solitary cart, or traveller on foot or horseback, but once we had left the last small market town, the country was for the most part bare, bleak and empty.

It was a little after four when the train stopped and I heard 'High Beck Halt. High Beck,' being called along the platform. I was the only one to alight and, after a moment, the train gathered steam again and pulled away. I stood, with my coat collar turned up against the bitter wind and snow blowing towards me down the line.

There was a single platform, and a small wooden building that served as waiting room and ticket office together, with a meagre fire of hard little coals sputtering in the iron grate. I sat down on the bench. There were cracks and chinks in the window frames and under the door through which the wind whistled and moaned, cold as a knife blade. But, with every mile further north I had come, the higher my spirits had lifted, and, seeing the open moors all around me, I had begun to feel a deep contentment. I was home, this was familiar, I belonged in these places, though they were as different as anywhere on earth could be from the landscapes in which I had lived as long as I could clearly remember. The wind, the cold, the loneliness of this place did not disturb me, nor was I at all troubled by any thoughts of what might lie ahead.

I sat for some while, deep in thought and dreams about Kittiscar. No one came into the waiting room, no train drew in at the station. Outside, it was growing darker.

The porter who had called out the stop had not re-appeared and, in the end, I was obliged to leave the shelter of the little room and go in search of him, to enquire when I could expect the next train that would stop at Raw Muck-lerby.

He was ensconced in a small box at the far end of the platform, an oil heater at his feet, and a fug of fumes and tobacco enveloping him. He opened the door only a slit in response to my knock, peering out through watery eyes.

When I put my question to him, he shook his head, and at that moment, the wind came blasting down the line, taking away his words, so that I had to put my head to the crack in the door and ask again.

I learned that I had been misinformed by an old railway guide. The branch line had closed 'long since'; there were no trains.

In the wind and gathering gloom, therefore, I hoisted up my bag, left the station, and set off, to walk the five miles across the road that led over the moor and thence, I was told, down the far side, to Raw Mucklerby.

I had walked many a long mile, in the bush, and over remote mountain tracks quite alone, I was fit and had a decent bump of direction, so the journey over these north of England moors held no fears for me. The dusk gathered and the night came on but after a mile or so, although it was cold, the wind began to veer and die down, and, looking up now and then, I caught a glimpse of a ragged patch of starry sky through the clouds, and some faint light shone through from a watery moon.

I came to a cross-roads at the highest point, and, although one of the arms was broken off and the lettering on the other faded, I felt sure I should continue ahead, following the gentle downward slope of the road. For a moment or two, though, I was forced to rest, setting my bag down on the ground beside me. The air smelled fresh and raw, of bare earth and the recent layer of snow, and I was not unhappy, but my limbs had begun to ache, I was very tired and I remembered how ill I had been only recently, and that I was still somewhat convalescent. Perhaps it had been foolish to walk this way tonight, and I had better have tried to find a bed somewhere at High Beck. But there was no point in turning back now, I was, as near as I could tell, at a halfway point, and I took up my bag again and moved off, for I thought that it would be more unwise to stand long in the bitter cold and risk catching another chill, than push myself onwards.

And then I saw the light, a steady single glow from what must be a window in some dwelling, perhaps half a mile away. It had the slight flickering look of an oil flame, and I stirred my step, grateful that I might be coming to some isolated cottage where I could perhaps get refreshment and a bed for the night. The path narrowed to little more than a track, and once or twice it seemed that the light was further away rather than closer, and once I hesitated, bewildered that I seemed to be going in the wrong direction altogether. But when I looked it was there again, wavering but clear, and I stumbled on, my legs numb, my neck and back sore, longing for any shelter, and a chance to rest.

My delight in the openness and wildness of the moor was giving way to nervousness that I might become lost on it, faint, or fall by accident, so far from help, but I summoned up all the strength I could from past experience of being in far more godforsaken places and forced myself to be calm and hopeful.

The strap of my bag was chafing and working loose and I stooped to adjust it, which took a little time. When I had finished, and was preparing to continue, I became quite suddenly, and horribly, certain that I was being followed, had been observed and stealthily pursued by someone the whole way. Also, looking up, I saw that the little light had disappeared. I stared and stared ahead, and all around me, turned a full circle, but there was only darkness, occasionally softened by the fleeting appearance and disappearance of the moon as the clouds parted and drew together again.

I was cold, I was exhausted, I felt ill, I had lost my way,

but these things I could have endured and overcome, they were real and not unfamiliar challenges. It was the fear that would prove my undoing, fear of the creeping and concealed shadow that had followed me here and was somewhere just out of sight in the gloom of the moor.

The wind keened faintly, a high, thin singing sound.

I hauled my bag onto my shoulder again and began to run. I ran for perhaps two hundred yards, in a blind panic, careless of the direction I was taking, consumed by a wild desperation to escape, though to what and from what I could not have told, for I was past rational, careful thought or deduction, I allowed fear to be my master on that open moor.

It was a sudden fall, as I caught my foot in a rabbit hole, that sent me crashing forward onto the ground and brought me to my senses. I lay stunned, the breath almost knocked out of me but, after a few seconds, I looked up at the sky and saw that it was clearer now, and that the stars were bright, the moon riding high and serene in their midst.

I sat up. All around me lay the quiet, rolling moor. I could see no one, had been followed by nothing, save creatures of my own imaginings. I was shivering and my ankle was wrenched, I was cold and weary, but the darkness and the countryside were not unfriendly. Was I so nervous and on edge then that I conjured up ghosts at every turn, was I as easily frightened as some little child or silly woman? I did not think so. I considered for a few moments. I *had* been watched, and followed, though not by anything real and visible, not by any human enemy. It had been there, darkening and souring the air, oppressing and terrifying me – and now, quite simply, it was gone, just as the malevolent presence in the library at Alton and at Pyre, and the sobbing of the boy, had been – and then not been.

I rose and somehow gathered my wits, pulled myself together, and went slowly on, following the path carefully again. From somewhere in the valley, a fox yelped, yelped again. Only a few yards further on, I saw the light once more, gleaming out from the window of a single, low cottage, and made towards it, with as brisk a step as I could muster, and a lightening heart.

The door opened directly onto a low-ceiling kitchen, with a black iron range and a rocking chair beside it, in which sat an old, toothless woman, wrinkled and gnarled like the root of some ancient tree, who wore a scarf about her head and mumbled her mouth as she rocked gently to and fro. But the one who admitted me was younger, ruddy-faced and cheerful, and at once offered me hot soup and good bread and a place beside the fire.

'I had planned to make the Inn at Raw Mucklerby,' I told her, 'but I have not long recovered from an illness and the walk across the moor tired me more than I expected. I confess I was heartily glad to see the light from your window and make for it. It is a bitter night.'

She nodded, filling up my bowl with the steaming, meaty soup.

'T'Ram Inn is another four mile on and th'track runs along by the stream for the last part and that's in full flood, you'd easily have toppled in in't dark.'

I listened entranced to the sound of her voice, and the broad, flat vowels she used, for the accent rang familiar to me, I felt at once at home with it.

'You're not from this way.'

'I have come today on the train from London. But in a sense I am near home. I have lived in many countries abroad, but it seems likely, I was born near here.'

She had sat down opposite to me at the table. She seemed interested in and well disposed towards me and I warmed to that, as well as with the relief of being here in safe shelter. The oil lamps were turned up, and the one in the window that had beckoned me here gleamed out bravely.

'It may be that you can be of help to me – that you know something of my family.'

'We've lived here at Goose Foot some twenty year, but before that my aunt and all hers before come from over at Scarsgate.'

'How far is that?'

'Seven mile.'

'Is it close to the place called Kittiscar?'

'No, no, that's over Rook's Crag way.' She spoke dismissively, as though it was foreign territory.

'Then perhaps you will not know my name. It is Monmouth – James Monmouth of Kittiscar.'

She shook her head, but then turned to the old woman, still rocking, rocking, her chair pulled up close to the hearth, and raised her voice a little.

'The gentleman's from up Kittiscar. You'd know them up there, aunty.'

The old woman opened her eyes and I saw that they were faded and sightless, filmed over with cataracts. But when she spoke her voice was strong.

'Kittiscar. That's a climb.'

'Would you know of Kittiscar Hall, Ma'am?'

'Aye.'

'You have been there?'

'Not been, no, though it's well enough known about.'

'What is known?'

'Tales. Haven't you heard the tales?'

'The gentleman has been abroad, he's only just back after years away.'

'Many years,' I said. 'Do you know anyone who lives at Kittiscar now?'

'Family, I daresay. Last I heard.'

The younger woman was shaking her head and spoke across the table to me in a half-whisper.

'Only she doesn't go out much now, it'd be way back, she's speaking of.'

[149]

'Never mind – I'm anxious to hear whatever she can tell me.'

'They've shut it up now, so I heard.'

'The Hall?'

''T chapel. No one goes nowadays.'

'Chapel?'

'Up at Kittiscar. That's where you mean.'

'I believe that a relative of mine still lives at the Hall. Miss Monmouth. It is my own name. Do you know her – or remember her in any way?'

'That was the name. Monmouth. That was some of them. We were kept out of it. Nobody would go.'

'You mean go to Kittiscar?'

'Kittiscar, aye. Only I know they did close it up, years back. We never went.'

I gave up, feeling the same frustration I had felt when old Mr Quincebridge had half-remembered my name. But now I was here and it scarcely mattered; I would go to see Miss Monmouth at the Hall, I hoped on the following day, and find out everything for myself. I only wondered about the chapel, now closed, and the vague mutterings the old woman made that they were 'kept out of it – never went'.

I was offered a bed in a tiny, cold room at the top of the steep staircase and accepted gladly, for my head ached now, and I felt a touch of fever about me again. I washed in a basin of cold water that was left for me, and drank some from a jug, and it tasted as sweet and clear as any I had ever known.

My bed was narrow and high, but I was warm enough beneath a great feather quilt, and I slept at once, and heavily, as cosy and safe as a little child, and woke the next morning, to a brilliant blue sky, and air, when I opened my casement window, blowing fresh and cold and clean from off the moor.

I did not know yet how long I would be staying in the area

and, although the woman expressed perfect willingness to let me keep on the room in the cottage, I felt it better to press on to the Inn where I could put up without inconveniencing anyone, and also, in a little more anonymity, though in that hope, I quickly realised, I was mistaken, for a stranger in any such remote country places provokes interest and comment at once and for miles around.

Raw Mucklerby was a dull little village lying in a dip along the main road, somewhat gloomy, and enclosed by the moors that rose behind it and which, when I arrived that morning, were in shadow, dun and featureless. But the Inn, though dark, with poky rooms, was comfortable and the landlord friendly.

On a sudden whim and for no reason I could have expressed clearly, I did not give him my full name, but merely asked for a room in the name of Mr James, of Chelsea, London.

'For how many nights would that be, sir?'

'I am as yet uncertain.'

'You have some business here then?'

'I – yes. In a sense. Interests, let us say.'

'Only that it's early on, for visitors. Nobody much gets up this way until t'summer months, when they come walking. And for t'shooting, later.'

Although I had eaten an excellent breakfast at the cottage and felt completely revived, I was wary and intended to conserve my strength more carefully. After unpacking my few belongings, I returned to the bar and sat there reading the paper and enjoying a pint of the local ale, sipping it slowly and with enjoyment. I was almost like a child saving up a treat, I anticipated something so momentous, such a wonderful revelation, at Kittiscar, that I held back from it a little longer.

The landlord busied himself about and did not intrude upon me. By twelve, several local men had come in, nodded to me, and then settled themselves, and their talk, in the broad, rough accent I was becoming familiar with, was of farming and other domestic matters. I ordered bread and cheese and sat enjoying it, listening to the voices as though to a background of murmuring music, until a name came ringing across the room to my ears.

'Kittiscar.'

I turned towards two burly men, seated at a table with their backs to the window, and, after a moment or two, crossed the room.

'Pardon me, sir . . .'

They greeted me in a friendly way.

'I could not help but overhear – I am a visitor of sorts, newly arrived here, but I have connections with the neighbourhood. You spoke of Kittiscar.'

'Aye.'

'You are from there?'

'No, from t'other side.'

'But you know the place?'

'I do.' The older man spoke, looking at me with a keener attention.

'I plan to walk up there later to visit Kittiscar Hall.'

'If you're a sightseer, you'll find it closed.'

'You mean empty?'

'Not so to say.'

'And what would there be to see?'

'Oh,' he said carefully, ''tis famous, in its way.'

'And grand once,' added the other, swirling round the dregs of his beer. I fancied there was more that they might impart if I pressed them, and I asked them if they knew the present owner.

'Miss Monmouth?'

'Yes.'

'You've business with her then?'

'I may have.'

'Well then.' He finished his ale methodically, and set down the tankard. 'You've a climb,' he said.

'So I'm told. Well, it's a good day for it.'

'Last I heard,' the other said, 't'old woman was bad. It could be true, *I* don't know. Nobody much goes.'

'I'm told that also.'

'She'd be old, that's certain, but as to her health . . .' He shrugged, and made to put on his hat, as they went towards the doorway. I was beginning to find the half-finished sentences and vague, dark, muttered hints about Kittiscar irritating.

'Then I had better go up there and find out for myself,' I said shortly. 'Good day to you.'

The bar was empty again, the landlord tidying away glasses. A shaft of sunlight illuminated the top of the moor, as I glanced through the window, softening and lightening the contours.

'I plan to return for supper,' I said, 'if it will be convenient.'

'To suit, sir.'

'Thank you.'

'Take no notice of what's said, is my advice to you. They like to make a bit of a mystery and it's true there've always been tales, but to my mind they're nowt else. And t'present lady's old, and not much seen. I had heard she was ill, but then, I've heard t'same on and off most winters.'

'Thank you. But, now it is spring,' I said, 'and I intend to visit her.'

'Good luck to you then – and there's pigeon pie for supper.'

He came to the front door of the Inn to set me on the road, indicating that I should retrace steps through the main part of the village and then strike directly east, over the moor.

I took my leave of him cheerfully, the sun high overhead and my step light, and began my walk to Kittiscar.

The previous night I had been exhausted and confused as to direction, now I felt fresh and vigorous and the way was not only signposted, I could see the path I was to follow, a clear, pale line up the slope and, when I reached the top, unrolling far ahead of me. Last night I had been afraid, feeling the old familiar terror of eyes upon me, footsteps behind. Now, I saw only beauty all around, the dark brown face of the moor bathed in sunlight, the deep shadows on the opposite slopes purple as grapes. I climbed steadily and the world was at my feet, I seemed to feel it turn beneath me. At one point, I saw an eagle, gliding on lazy, outspread wings above the highest peak; at another, when I sat resting on the short turf, larks spiralled up and up, pouring out their streams of pure song high above my head. The grass smelled pungently of some herb as I got up, the sun was warm now on my back and the track rose steeply, steadily away. But I had no tiredness at all in my limbs today. This was a world in which I felt at home, these were places I knew in my bones; I had seen them before, I felt exhilarated beyond expression.

It was six miles before I saw a wooden signpost. Kittiscar ½. The track became a rough paved road again and dipped steeply between high banks before rising up towards the grey cottages. At the point where the lane was lowest, a stream flowed over pebbles right across my path, and, when I reached it, I stood transfixed, looking down into the transparent water, for here, surely, I had stood, this I knew, the gentle sound of the running water was long familiar.

I went on very slowly, up the last slope, towards the houses. They were plain, grey stone and set right up to the lane. Here and there, a gateway led to a yard. A hen strutted. A mangy cat sat, eyes half-closed, on a window-ledge. But there was no one about, and no sounds at all, save for some birdsong, and the far-off barking of a dog.

Several times I stopped to stare at closed doors, at gates, at fences, willing the door to the past to swing open.

At the top of the one lane that was all of Kittiscar, a single cottage was set a little back and apart from the rest, and beside it stood a separate stone building with an open doorway. Within, all was dark as a cave, and for a few seconds until my eyes adjusted themselves from the bright daylight outside, I saw nothing. But I smelled, smelled the pungent, ancient smell of horse, of dry hay and blackened iron and cold, damp stone, and another acrid smoky smell. The stable was empty, the forge cold and lifeless. But, if I closed my eyes, I saw it all, the white core of the furnace and the showering, golden sparks, heard the whinnying of the horses and the clang of hammer on anvil, and the blacksmith whistling through his teeth, heard the sizzling hiss of water onto white hot metal. I was a small boy again, staring into the blacksmith's den, half captivated, half afraid, wanting, but never daring, to go closer. And it was here, here in this doorway.

I opened my eyes. The forge was long cold, the floor bare and dirty, the metal restraining hoop and the iron hay rack rusted over. There was silence.

I shivered and retreated, back into the lane.

My feelings then are difficult to convey, they changed and shifted from moment to moment, like the fleeting sunlight as it moved over the moors. I had no clear or definite memories, but I recalled, as I stood still in that deserted place, a sense of dissolution, of loss and sadness. I had been here, of that I was now quite certain, and I thought I had been happy, but then things had changed, shadows had fallen.

It was all vague and unsubstantial, but my mood now was considerably affected.

I walked on up the steep slope of the village lane, and came out beyond the last cottages and a farm. Below, I could see for miles, across the whole, beautiful, bare moor-

[155]

land landscape. But to my right was a path, leading to an open gateway between overhanging trees. I turned and walked up to it. On the gate, just discernible, though faded and half worn away, was the name KITTISCAR HALL.

My heart seemed to be squeezed tight within my chest and then to leap, almost to stop, as I looked at the old letters.

The path, narrow and overgrown, though it had clearly once been a drive, went up through the trees into what seemed dense woodland, but I followed it, and saw that it was cleared of undergrowth after some distance, and clearly not unused.

At Pyre, it had already been early spring, with the snow-drops and crocuses almost over, and the daffodils ready to break, but here in the north there was scarcely a sign of it, the trees were still quite bare and the grass shrivelled and flowerless.

I heard nothing save my own soft footsteps and once or twice the sudden rustle of branches as some creature fled away from my approach. The path climbed a little, and then opened out.

The house was before me, a plain, old country manor. It was large, and dark, and it was neglected, the paint peeling at the windows, paving cracked and sunken. It seemed empty, the shutters closed in several of the upper windows, and the whole place silent.

I had expected it to be familiar to me, to give a cry of recognition. But I did not, I might never have seen it before.

I wandered along the side path that led to an entrance through a high wall, where once a gate had stood. But the hinges were broken off and the entrance gaped. I went through. And came into a derelict and empty garden, with a small pond in the centre, that must once have held fish and been bright with lilies, but whose water was stagnant now. Beyond this was a yard, empty outbuildings, disused stables, with cobblestones sprouting grass and slippery with moss. I crossed it to a second gate, set in a high wall, but this was firmly in place, padlocked and held with a rusty chain. I peered through. I saw an ancient yew hedge, over which the tangle of an old rose had climbed and scrambled, and a brick path leading around the edge, towards a broken stone seat at the far end. Behind it, elm trees rose, with dozens of crows' nests in the high, still branches.

In the centre of the garden, on the overgrown grass, was a leaden statue; it was of a graceful boy, raised on one foot, with an arm outstretched. The forefinger which pointed up was broken off. And, then, another flash of clear memory came to me; I knew the statue, every curve and line of it, I had stood in that garden, I had woven stories to myself around the figure of that solitary, leaden boy.

I turned and looked back to the house, and then I saw that a thin plume of smoke rose from the chimney. Someone was living here then, Miss Monmouth must be at home, an old recluse, who had been left in the midst of this wilderness that had once been a great house.

I also saw, to my left, another path leading off towards a clump of yew trees, and at the far end could glimpse the wall and roof of what seemed to be a building, rising slate-grey and sombre against the sky.

But, for the moment, my interest was in the house, and its inhabitant. I made my way back across the yard and through the open archway, to the front door.

Some cloud had blown up from the west now, covering the sun; it was dark and gloomy, as I pulled on the bell and heard it echo within. No place for an old woman alone. I myself would have been glad of any cheerful voice or presence, glad of any human company at that moment.

I rang again, and eventually heard footsteps, and the sound of bolts being drawn back. I stood my ground, but with rising apprehension, as the door of Kittiscar Hall was opened.

CHAPTER FOURTEEN

I said, 'I have come to see Miss Monmouth.'

She nodded, and moved back, to indicate, in silence, that I should step into the hall.

My feelings as I did so are indescribable. I stared in wonder, slowly all about me, at the heavy tapestries covering the stone walls and the dark pictures that loomed above me, at the oak doors and uneven, flagged floor, the huge hearth, with the coat of arms carved over it, and, as I stood there, the gate swung wide at last and the past came flooding towards me like a river, so that I almost drowned in it. I was a small boy again, standing here gazing about me in awe and apprehension, and clutching onto old Nan's hand – involuntarily now I clutched my fingers and felt it, dry and with knobs at the joints and a roughened palm.

The smell of the house, a mingling of stone and damp, ancient wood and dust, was the same, overwhelming, pungent smell, I had known so well, then.

'If you would like to come this way, and wait a few minutes. I will take you up directly.'

The woman was whey-faced and soft-voiced, without the local accent. She wore a plain apron, and rusty black dress, her hair was streaked grey. I went through the door that she held open, but she did not follow me in, only closed it behind her, and went off.

I was in a long, panelled drawing room, with leaded windows, the ledges lined with plants, old and untamed, struggling, climbing, creeping things thick with dust, that crowded out any light. There were more worn tapestries and dark pictures and in the centre of the room a long refectory table lined with pewter candlesticks, and an oak sideboard laid with heavy pewter jugs and dishes. The floor was stone-flagged, save for some threadbare carpet beneath the table, and laid before the cold, empty hearth. It was a cheerless room, overbearing and gloomy, and quite without comfort, soft chairs or window-seats or small personal possessions. I had memories of it, the same feelings swept over me as in the entrance hall, memories of being intimidated by this room, and of trying to shrink back from it, towards the door again and the safe, bright, outside world.

I walked up and down, my own steps hard and clear on the stone floor. It might have had no occupant for months, and seemed to have little to do with everyday, human existence. I supposed that Miss Monmouth had been more ill than was generally known, perhaps for a long time, and was now bedridden and no longer able to use these great, formal rooms.

The woman who opened the door had seemed quite unsurprised by my appearance. It was possible, of course, that word of my arrival had already sped around the countryside, but more likely that Miss Monmouth had spoken of my letter, in which I had proposed to come to Kittiscar.

She returned after some while, and gestured for me to follow her toward the dark staircase, and as I did so my head was crowded with the questions I wanted to ask about the house, and my relative, but, most of all, about myself and my memories of childhood, for it seemed likely that she would be the only one to enlighten me, whether or not we had ever met or were, perhaps, only very distantly related.

As we reached the landing, and turned, I saw a passageway leading off ahead, presumably to another part of the house, and, looking down it, I felt again most vividly what I had been dimly aware of that night in the Cross Keys Inn, and knew that at the end of this passage lay a room reached through a beaded curtain, on the far side of which would be sitting an old woman in a gypsy shawl, with a parrot swinging in a cage that hung from a hook beside her. I shuddered, remembering, though now there was nothing, there was only darkness and a closed door.

I would have asked questions, would have said, 'I have been here. Who was it? Whose room? Who lived here then?' But I saw that the woman was waiting for me – and, besides, she would almost certainly not have known.

I turned and followed her, our steps sounding hollow on the bare oak boards of the landing, until we stopped outside a door.

So, now, I was at last to see Miss Monmouth, my only living relative. My mouth was dry, my heart beating hard in my chest.

It was a bedroom, long and low-ceilinged, with bare floorboards and some simple, dark pieces of old country furniture. The shutters were closed, so that at first I hesitated, unable to see into the gloom. But the woman stepped quietly across to the windows, and folded the shutter back, and, glancing out, I saw that the sky had clouded over and was heavy and blue-black.

Then, she left the room, closing the door very softly behind her, and I was alone with my relative.

A carved oak bed stood opposite to me, without curtains or pillows, and I went forward quietly, preparing my first, gentle greeting, for I was anxious not to startle or worry an old woman.

[161]

She wore a bone-coloured cotton gown and her grey hair was pulled back from her forehead and dressed in a thin little plait which rested in the crook of her neck. Her arms were folded, hands together on top of one another. The flesh, what little there was – for she seemed immensely old, and wasted – had sunk back into the hollows of her eyes and mouth and below the cheekbones, and her nose jutted up, hooked and sharp as the beak of a hawk. Her eyes were closed, her skin was dull and waxen.

Miss Monmouth was dead, and I, the visitor, had been allowed in to view her corpse, and pay it my first, and last, respects.

It was only by a supreme effort of will that I managed to stand my ground firmly, for my limbs felt as if they would dissolve, the whole room seemed unsteady, the floor to shift like the sea beneath my feet.

In panic, I looked up from the dreadful still figure laid out before me, and my eyes found the wall behind the bed. On it was an elaborately carved mirror, with faded and cracked gilding, and dark streaked glass, the exact counter-part of the mirror that had been hanging in the bedroom at Alton, and as I stared into it, my own face, pale and with terrified, haunted eyes, looked back at me dimly, through a grey, swirling mist.

Rain rattled suddenly against the casements, and in the distance, from over the moors, came the sound of thunder.

CHAPTER FIFTEEN

To my sole surviving relative,
Mr James Monmouth

The woman had returned, and led me back down through that oppressive old house, not to the gloomy room in which I had first waited, but to a small parlour, where a bleak fire had been recently lit and smouldered sulkily in the grate. The room smelled of damp, everything seemed as though undisturbed for years, but there were at least a few trinkets and books to soften the bareness. A tray, with a decanter of sherry and some plain cake, stood on a small table. Propped up against it was the letter.

'So you knew that I was coming here – you know my name.'

The woman inclined her head, but I noticed that she stood back from me, as if afraid, and her eyes were wary, she did not readily meet my glance.

'Miss Monmouth received my letter.'

'She did.'

'But, by then, I suppose that she was too ill to reply?'

She cleared her throat, her hands fidgeting on her apron.

'She'd been ill a good long while. Only . . .'

'Yes?'

'It shook her.'

'My letter?'

'There was no thought that anyone else was left.'

'Indeed not. I know of no other relative myself – that is why I am so anxious to come here and find – find Miss Monmouth passed away. There is so much we might have talked about, so much that she would have told me. I know little about my family – and Kittiscar – my own self. Perhaps you . . .'

'No,' she said quickly. 'I came from away. To Miss Monmouth. She was to be looked after. But none of the rest of it is my concern.'

'Did she speak of me to you?'

She indicated the letter beside the tray. 'What she wanted to say she said there – though she was dying then, and knew it. But clear in her mind. When you've taken your refreshment and read what she had to say, I expect you will let me have your instructions.'

'Instructions?'

'As to the arrangements.'

'Oh, I would want to leave everything to you or to anyone else local who knew her. I don't expect to interfere with the funeral in any way.'

She nodded, unsmiling. 'And, as to the rest, perhaps you will say in due course.'

She turned quickly, seeming anxious to be out of my presence, so that I thought it best not to try and question her further.

I poured myself a full glass of the dark sweet sherry, and drank it off at once, and took another, for my nerves were not yet steady, I had not at all recovered from the shock of finding myself alone with the dead body of Miss Monmouth.

[164]

Outside, the rain was still heavy, and the thunder prowling low about the house.

I sat in the straight-backed chair, my glass close to hand, and took up the letter.

It was written in ink, in a shaky, old-fashioned but clearly legible hand. The paper itself was headed in the same form as the envelope.

To my sole surviving relative, James Monmouth,

Kittiscar is yours. I am sorry for you. There has been no trouble for me, being a woman. You are not known to me. I had never been told.

There is no fortune, they left us nothing save the house, which came back into the family at last. It is as I found it. You must order things as you will for I am weary of it.

I have left instructions for my burial at Rook's Crag. Not here. I could not rest here.

    E. Monmouth

There is little of interest to tell about the events of the following two days. From the woman, I learned that tentative arrangements for the funeral had been made – it was to take place in the nearest market town, followed by burial there – and I confirmed them hastily, not wishing to interfere at all, or put forward any alternative plans of my own.

I returned to the Inn at Raw Mucklerby that afternoon. There seemed nothing for me to do and I felt curiously flat and dispirited. I had inherited Kittiscar, my family home. I had some dim childhood memories of visiting it, and of being in the village and the countryside around, presumably with whoever the old woman was who had looked after me. No one seemed to remember or be interested in me, I had no information at all about my parents or the rest of my family, and knew nothing of what had happened to them, and suddenly, lying listlessly on my bed at the Inn, I felt as though I had been excitedly following some path, with great difficulty, led on, led on – only to arrive at a dead end, a blank wall. Nothing.

Is this all? I asked. Apparently it was.

It seemed likely that everything that had happened to me, the odd, frightening incidents, things seen and heard, had been products either of coincidence, which had nothing to do with me, but which I had simply hit upon by purest chance, or else of an over-fevered and disturbed imagination, a heightened sensibility caused by illness and the strain and strangeness of arriving in another country, at the end of the old familiar life and the abrupt beginning of a new.

I was disappointed and yet perhaps also in some ways relieved. Things had an ordinary explanation – or none; my past was without mystery, my future set to be dull and uneventful. So be it.

Miss Monmouth's funeral was a plain affair, in a neat, well-kept little church. A few more people than I had anticipated were gathered there, and I noticed that in the church I was avoided, and left to sit alone at the front, and at the graveside, too, I was apart, and the object of covert glances. But that was scarcely surprising – I was an interesting stranger in a close-knit, somewhat isolated community, being treated with wary courtesy and respect as the chief mourner and only living relative of the deceased.

But I exchanged some friendly words with the officiating clergyman, an old retired Canon, who had, he said, visited my relative occasionally in the past few years.

'And now,' I said, 'I hope, you will visit me.' The others had left the churchyard and we were standing alone together beside the lych gate. He frowned, as if he had not understood.

'I am Miss Monmouth's heir – the only member of the family left, or so I suppose. I have inherited Kittiscar.'

'But I take it you will not be living there. You are come from abroad, and I . . .'

'Yes, but my days of travelling and living in foreign countries are over. I came back to England determined to settle, long before I knew of Kittiscar or my connections with it. I had felt something, memories and recollections, were drawing me back home and, now, home is to be Kittiscar. I shall return to London to clear my belongings, and some few business matters there, but then I shall return and take over Kittiscar Hall.'

In truth, I had not known that this was indeed my plan, had made no decision, until I heard myself speak then. But I was convinced at that moment that it would be so, and was indeed what I most wanted.

The man was looking distraught, his mouth working, his eyes not meeting mine, as if he were desperately trying to nerve himself to speak, and torn between the desire to do so and the anxiety he clearly felt about the matter.

'There is something wrong?' I asked.

'I . . . no, no. That is . . .'

'Come.'

'Then – oh, think hard, Mr Monmouth, think it over most carefully, I urge you. It is a lonely life here – and alien to you – Kittiscar is – not perhaps the place for a man in the prime of active life, on his own, knowing no one . . . surely London and other interests will call you, stimulate you more . . .' He burbled on, his fingers plucking at the edge of his surplice, which blew about him in the wind. I shivered and turned up my coat collar.

'No,' I said boldly, beginning to make my way out of the gate, 'London holds no interest at all for me. I am not a city man. I have come home, and here I shall stay.' I proffered my hand. My own grip was firm. His was not, his hand was trembling and uncertain in mine. I looked at him and saw kindness in his old eyes, kindness and deep concern for me. And fear.

[167]

But he said nothing, only walked with me to the road-side, and watched me leave, before returning to the church.

At the corner, I glanced back. The wind was blowing bitterly cold off the moors, and rippling through the branches of the yews in the graveyard. Underneath them, and looking away from me, towards the freshly mounded earth of my relative's grave, stood the boy, ragged, pale, thin, and quite as clear, real, visible to me as he had always been.

I averted my head before he could turn and look at me, and quickened my step away from the place.

CHAPTER SIXTEEN

I supposed that the mourners at the funeral had simply dispersed back to their own homes. If there was any gathering, to eat and drink and reminisce, I had not been invited to it.

I returned to the Inn, ate some cold meat and bread for lunch, among the local men, read a paper, wrote a few letters, including one describing everything in detail and relieving myself of many of my pent-up feelings, to the Quincebridges. Indeed, I thought altogether longingly of Pyre and their company and my time there, and even of my rooms at Number Seven, Prickett's Green. Here, I felt lonely and strange and, if I regretted what I had said to the parson about taking over my inheritance at Kittiscar Hall, it was not because his palpable anxiety had influenced me, and certainly not because of the reappearance of the boy, but simply because of the depressed sense of anti-climax that continued with me now.

In the end, shortly after three that afternoon, I decided to go up again to Kittiscar, to look over the Hall, and begin to familiarise myself with it, make plans and see if I could even begin to feel at home there.

The wind was blowing in my face, making the climb over

the moor a hard one, but the views from the summit were glorious in the afternoon sun, and I felt so exhilarated by the great openness of this northern countryside that I had begun to love, that my spirits lifted as I went, hearing the plaintive bleating of the sheep and the birds' cries all around me.

I had a list of questions forming in my head as I walked. Principally, I wondered whether any land went along with the Hall, or if I might possibly buy some to call my own, to have some sheep and rough cover for shooting, and a stream in which to fish. I saw the house transformed gradually into a comfortable gentleman's home, not grand (and, in any case, I had no money for grandeur) but welcoming, with my books and a good dog, and the garden brought back to itself, a place to which I could welcome visitors. Perhaps somewhere at the back of my mind was even the thought that one day Kittiscar would be a home to which I might bring a wife, so that it would be truly alive with family happiness and the sound of children.

Such warm sentiments did not seem to me in the least foolish, so inspired and invigorated was I by my walk over the moor and the thought of my inheritance.

The village street was as silent and deserted as before, almost as if it had been abandoned and left to crumble, for all the smoke rising thinly here and there from cottage chimneys. But I refused to let the eerie quietness and emptiness dampen my spirits now, and I intended to walk up a few paths and knock on some doors, in the weeks to come.

Making my way slowly through the silent, neglected gardens at the Hall, I realised that I was already beginning to feel quite differently towards the place, felt mounting excitement, saw possibilities in every corner, and longed for it to be restored to life again. Standing in front of the lead statue of the boy, which seemed so friendly and familiar to me, I pledged rather fervently that I would work, give my whole life, to make Kittiscar a place of happiness and prosperity once again, no matter what the cost. There was no fortune, my relative said in her letter. But somehow, I determined, money should be found, I would work, things would be done. Above all, I needed to enthuse those around me, bring people up here, enlist their help in making Kittiscar the centre of a thriving village again.

I had wondered if the house might be empty, but the woman let me in almost as soon as my hand touched the bell, though she stared at me blankly and, for a few seconds, did not step back to let me into the hall. I said, 'I am sorry it is a little late, but I have come again simply to go around the Hall, not to change or disturb anything just now, of course,' I added, seeing her guarded, faintly hostile expression, 'out of respect for my relative.'

'You will not find anything of interest. It is an old neglected place, and Miss Monmouth had been very ill for some time. She confined herself to one part of the house.'

'Yes. Nevertheless, I should like to see and begin to form plans.'

'As you wish. Of course, it is yours to take away what you choose.'

'Oh, I do not imagine I shall take anything away, not for a good while at least. I shall leave all the furnishings and so forth as they are until I have a feel of the place, and I have little of my own to bring. As I think you know, I came from years spent abroad, and had no home. My possessions are very few.'

She continued to stare at me but now a look of almost horror crossed her features when she spoke, her voice a whisper.

'You surely are not planning to live here at Kittiscar?'

'Why certainly I am! I have no other home. I am the heir to the house, am I not?'

'But you cannot – surely you will not.'

[171]

'Why do you say so?'

'Because . . . because you are a Monmouth and a man.'

A sentence from my relative's letter came to my mind. 'I am sorry for you. There has been no trouble for me, *being a woman.*' I felt a clutching sensation in the pit of my stomach. Whatever was wrong, whatever I had been warned about in the past and again now, had to do with Kittiscar Hall and the Monmouth family in reference to its male line. For a moment, I wanted to have it out with her there and then, to hear the full truth. But I did not ask. I dismissed it. It was some story, an old tale such as often attached itself to an old house. Some nonsense.

I went into every room at Kittiscar Hall that day. The sun was shining into those at the back of the house and, when I opened the shutters and pulled all the heavy, dingy curtains to one side, light flooded in. The furniture was dark and in many cases ugly carved oak, but although it was dusty and the whole place wore the same threadbare, neglected air, I felt heartened that the decay was not by any means far gone and sure that I could live in the place more or less as it was, once it had been given an airing. I pushed hard on the windows, but only one or two would open. Still, it let in some measure of fresh air and late sunshine here and there.

My relative had had precious few personal belongings; her clothes and linen were in the bedroom in which I had seen her body, together with a few trinkets and books. Otherwise she had left no trace of herself; it was almost as though she had lived as a caretaker of the place and made no impress of herself upon it.

I went everywhere, from attics to damp, unlit cellar, and down every passage and into every nook and cranny, and I felt nothing in the slightest degree fearful or dreadful there; I saw no ghosts, heard no strange sounds. It was merely dismal and gloomy, dark and curiously lifeless. My sense of familiarity with it had been dimmed. I had no further, clearer memories and could only suppose that my childhood visits had been fleeting and very early. Certainly, I was sure now that I had never lived here. But my sense of the terrible woman in her room at the end of the passage was vivid still, and when I passed there I shrank back involuntarily, and felt the strong presence of someone beside me whose hand I clutched and in whose skirts I had hidden.

At last, I returned to the attic, wanting to look over to the open moor again, and wondering if I might make these my own quarters, at least for the beginning of my life here. I could furnish these empty rooms with a few of my own simple things, and there was a brightness and airiness up here that was absent from the rest of the Hall.

It was as I gazed through the grimy casement at the rooks swirling about in the tree tops and the rising purple line of the moor ahead, that, glancing to my left, I saw the grey stone walls of the building I had glimpsed down the path between trees on my first visit here, and now I saw that the roof went to a point, at the top of which was an old bell, and realised that I was looking onto the chapel belonging to the Hall, to which the men at the Inn had referred.

The woman was nowhere to be seen, and the house was quite silent, as I ran down through it and out at a side door I had discovered earlier led to a small inner courtyard, and thence through a wooden gate in the wall, directly to the overgrown grassy paths and shrubs at the back of the Hall. From here, I found my way, at times up to my knees in undergrowth and briars, to the path under the trees, and followed it, with a mingled feeling of curiosity and apprehension.

The sun had just set and the sky was darkening. To the east, I saw heavy clouds banking up.

Once, I looked back. I could see the side of the Hall and

its boundary wall, and one chimney, but there were no windows and I could not have been seen.

From somewhere, a blackbird pinked a sudden, angry warning, before fluttering low through the undergrowth. The rooks were cawing around the tops of the elms as they circled, settling down to roost. But the wind had dropped, and the air was quite still and even close along this narrow, overgrown path, through the overhanging trees.

Then, I came out into a small clearing, and the chapel was immediately in front of me, dark, still, and silent, grim in the last of the light. An iron grille stood in front of the low door, which I half expected to find padlocked, but as I touched it, it gave way at once, swinging open with a grating sound on its rusty hinges.

I hesitated before the wooden door, feeling suddenly cold and as though a shadow had fallen over me, and someone unseen but hostile was standing just a few feet away on my left side.

But I steeled myself, summoning up every ounce of resolution I possessed, for I knew that I was surely only responding to some melancholy mood of the time of day and the fading light, and the loneliness of my situation in this weird spot. At last, taking a deep breath and muttering an impulsive prayer for protection, I put my hand to the iron ring that served as a handle to the chapel door. It turned easily. I hesitated, before boldly pushing open the wooden door.

CHAPTER SEVENTEEN

It was the smell that struck me first, a sour, penetrating smell of cold damp stone and earth; there might have been no air let into the building for a hundred years.

Two shallow steps led down into the body of the chapel, which was small and rectangular, with high, narrow windows in plain glass, and a bare stone altar at the far end.

I stepped down warily, and almost fell, as the flagstones shifted and tipped unevenly. The floor was cracked and sinking, and here and there great cracks ran, and bare earth showed through. The walls were stained with damp and mould, the pews unsteady so that as I reached out to the nearest one it rocked slightly. A small pile of prayer books and hymnals was mildewed over and, in front of the altar, the remains of a cloth had almost rotted away. But, on the wall, a lion and unicorn board stood out, the painted colours darkened but the form and gilding still clear.

It was a drear little place, stifling and airless, speaking only of ruin and decay. I walked slowly down the aisle, noticing that the floorboards beneath the pew benches were rotten and blackened, the stone ledges crumbling away, and that there was a rubble of old twigs and grasses on part of the floor, where a bird's nest had fallen through a hole in the roof.

At the far end, I noticed a low archway in the stone and went cautiously over to it, before I realised that steps led down into darkness, and recoiled, for the stench rising from below was foul, of decay and death as well as of the cold and neglect of years.

Then, I saw that the stones at my feet at this end of the chapel were engraved.

Here lies Joshua Monmouth
Born 1583   Died 1613
Here lyeth Digby Monmouth and his sons
Here lies . . . Here lies . . . Here lies . . .

I traced out every name. My ancestors were at my feet, how many of them I could not tell, for many of the stones were too broken and worn away to decipher.

Then I came to a last stone, close to the steps, and bending down, for it was growing darker now, traced with my finger the outline of the words.

Here lies George Edward Pallentire Monmouth

I stood. Every tomb, of every Monmouth of Kittiscar. Every male, for there was no woman buried here.

And then, my eye was caught by a plaque let into the wall, altogether more elaborate and flourishing in style. I went closer and read it.

This memorial erected to
Conrad Vane of Kittiscar.
Imperator
18–

As I stood trembling before it, horrified, confused and yet somehow at last in dawning understanding, I heard a sound and, turning, saw the door of the chapel, which I had left open, begin slowly, softly to close. I ran to it, reached out and grabbed the handle, as I stumbled up the uneven steps. But rattle it, twist and turn and wrench it as I might, it would not yield to me. The door was not only closed but locked, and I locked in by it, trapped in the darkening, empty chapel. I fell and grasped the nearest pew, clutched at it and sat down, shaking and terrified. There was still light left in the sky, I looked up and saw it, a beautiful deep blue-grey, tantalising, beyond the high windows, the light of the outside world, which I could not reach. I got up and ran frantically round, clambered up onto another pew to see if I might get a purchase on the stones and climb up to the windows somehow, but of course I could not, there was no foothold of any kind and, in any case, the windows were barred.

I waited, trying to calm myself and to order my thoughts, but the feelings I had were more than those ordinary, inevitable ones that would have overcome any man in that situation. Outside the door I had sensed a watcher, a presence at my shoulder. Now, I felt it again. I knew that at my side was a presence, a looming, leering, triumphant, malevolent presence that had lured me here, where I was intended finally to be, a Monmouth among others long dead and buried and decayed.

I dared not turn my head or look over my shoulder. Instead I looked up and ahead.

He was standing at the open entrance to the crypt, I saw him, shadowy, hunched close to the stone wall. His body half concealed by the dark, heavy clothes he wore, his face slightly averted.

But I knew him, knew him from the seductive, smiling expression of decadence and silken cunning, knew him for my tormentor and betrayer, as well as for the murderer of my young innocent relative, and the corrupter of how many others, knew him for the way he had tempted me and led me on, from so long ago, at first all eager and willing to follow, and innocent, too, later bewitched and perverse,

[177]

half-reluctant, half-afraid, but nevertheless in thrall. That end of the dank, crumbling chapel seemed to exude Vane's presence, as the walls had exuded him everywhere he had pursued me.

I was angry and filled with hatred, but most of all I was afraid, paralysed with fear of that dreadful, ghastly presence in the shadows.

The light was fading fast now, I could scarcely see ahead. Then, I heard the noise, the breathing, as I had heard it before; the walls seemed to heave in and out like a dreadful pair of spongy lungs, and to puff out foul air as they did so. I stood up suddenly, reaching towards the last dying light from the sky, through the windows above me, looked wildly all around that chapel for some escape, and then I cried out, 'What do you want? *What do you want of me?*' My voice rang round the stone walls and echoed mockingly back to me, and then I fell silent, and bent forwards, sobbing, my head on my hands, in fear and despair.

When I had gained control of myself again, and raised my head, fearfully, the place was pitch black and deathly silent. I peered forwards, and saw nothing, sat still, straining my ears, and heard nothing . . . He had gone.

Then, from far away, beyond the chapel walls, and the closed door, from somewhere outside in the night, among the trees or in the bare, deserted garden, or even out on the moor, faintly, I heard the boy sobbing, sobbing in all his young loneliness and anguish and despair, the same that I now felt, trapped and cornered and perhaps doomed, as he had been, for who would find me, who would know that I had come here? I had been lured to Kittiscar and to my inheritance, the last surviving male member of my family, and was no more intended to go free than my pale, tormented boy, or any of the others now lying under the slabs below my feet.

That night was the most terrible I had ever spent, or pray

to God I will ever spend. Waves of evil and malevolence crept towards me and receded again, like waves of some sinister silent sea; the smell, a foetid stench of decay, rose like a poison, puffed out into the air, hissing gassily from corners, so that I almost choked upon it, and then it was gone again, and all was cold, empty stone and earth. I heard sounds, whispers and movements behind me; a dreadful cold crept up through my body, a more intense and penetrating cold than the mere cold of the night in that unheated, ancient building.

I seemed suspended in time, the night went on for a hundred years, and yet there was no time, or at least no movement of time forward. I was in a half-daze, half-delirium; shaking, I lay down on a pew and hid my head beneath my arms and again and again I returned to hammer and rattle and bang upon the door, and wrench in rage and impotence at the handle, but it was immovable, as if it had been locked and rusted for centuries.

How I clung onto life I do not know. By dawn, a sour, pale, ghostly dawn, breaking upon the cold stones and my shattered, cowed, exhausted frame, I was indeed half-dead, half-mad.

If the old man, the Canon, had not ridden out as soon as it was breaking light, to seek me out, because he had lain awake half the night in dreadful fear for me, then I would have been very shortly beyond salvation.

He found me, on that fresh, cold, dew-filled morning, crouched on the floor of the chapel, my arms crossed over my head, like a terrified animal, after he had turned the handle of the chapel door and, finding it unlocked and easily opened at a touch, come cautiously in.

I was taken across the moor, wrapped in a rough blanket, to the cottage hospital, where I was nursed with honest care and skill until my body at least was out of danger. But it was many weeks before my mind began to heal and, in all that time, the old Canon visited me daily and sat with me and prayed over me, patiently and with single-minded concern and, at last, I began to emerge from my nightmare and terrors, and face the world again.

But I was a broken man, scarred and damaged in the deepest recesses of my being beyond repair, and even now, as I write this some forty years later, I know the frailty of my sanity and health.

I learned a very little more about Kittiscar and my family, and the curse that had been laid upon it centuries before by an ancestor of Conrad Vane, as evil as he and upon whom he seems to have modelled himself, and only thanked God that I had escaped, with my life, by some great blessing or good fortune. Kittiscar, the Hall, the village and the land around, had been wrenched from my family; the Vanes had triumphed, by cunning, devilish means, and, reign after reign of subtle terror, they had pursued and corrupted and hounded every male Monmouth, including my own father, as, finally, Conrad Vane had sought and lured and ensnared me, even from beyond the grave.

All these things I learned or pieced together, step by slow step, over many months – for, at first, I could not speak or think of any of it, and later what little the Canon himself knew he was reluctant to tell, for fear of unhinging my mind again and destroying my health permanently.

He was a sterling friend to me, a saviour, indeed, wholly good, simple, and stalwart. What strength and peace of mind I regained and now possess I owe to him and his unselfish, prayerful devotion. I was alive. The hauntings ceased altogether and have never returned.

I only worried, from time to time, about the boy, whose distress and grief I felt I had not assuaged, for all that he was now entirely absent and silent. But, very gradually, even he began to fade from the forefront of my mind, and at last I ceased to think of him.

Sir Lionel and Lady Quincebridge travelled north to visit me several times and, towards the end of that year, took me back with them to Pyre, where I remained, convalescent and frail, for many months, wholly dependent upon their loving kindness, and deeply, humbly aware of my good fortune.

Eventually, under Sir Lionel's guidance, I took up the study of the Law, and that has been my satisfactory profession these past years. I never married, never found the confidence and strength to found that happy family of which I had had visions at Kittiscar, and so I am the last of the Monmouths, the family dies when I die, as the Vanes also died; there will be no survivors, no victors, so that the curse and the evil and the hauntings are certain to be at an end then, and the world a better place in the absence of us all.

I never returned to Kittiscar, nor knew anything about it, from that dawn when I was dragged away from the chapel, half-dead. What became of the Hall, who took it, if anyone, I have no wish ever to know.

Sir Lionel and Lady Quincebridge went abroad to the Mediterranean, for his health, and Pyre was sold. From time to time, I visited them, until first his and then, quite recently, her death. Perhaps, if ever I might have married a woman, it would have been Viola Quincebridge, but she was quite devoted to his memory, and nothing was ever spoken between us.

I am quite alone now. I have lived the last forty years in fear and never told it. Only now, at the last, I am moved to write this, and so lift the burden from my back and lay it down.

But I was surely not meant to live so long, nor ever in such comparative safety and contentment as have been granted to me, and for which I heartily thank God.

James Monmouth

POSTSCRIPT

Sir James Monmouth's story remained vividly in my mind for the whole of the day after I had sat up reading it. I could scarcely concentrate upon my work, and several times caught myself standing still and gazing unseeingly ahead, its details and incidents unfolding before my mind's eye.

I vowed that, when I returned it to him at the Club, I would sit with the old man and keep him company a little, recognising now how lonely he must be, and even made a vague plan to take him down to Norfolk, to be cosseted for a weekend by Ann.

I was never to do so.

Business took me to Scotland for the better part of the next week, and, when I returned, I went to the Club at the end of a tiring day, to relax over a drink.

I was greeted almost at once by the news which had been the talk of the place since the previous evening – Sir James Monmouth was dead. Sideham had found him, sitting in a chair in a corner of the library, in the hour just before dawn, an expression of what was said to have been amazement upon his face. He had been slumped down in the great wing chair and gone unnoticed when the porter had gone into the room last thing before retiring.

There was another story too, they were talking about it in the bar when I joined them, very much in need of their company. There had been some sort of disturbance, perhaps an intruder in the Club; the night porter had been alerted by it, while dozing in his chair in the lodge, and gone to investigate. Nothing had been taken, and no damage done. But he had surprised a boy, a ragged urchin, of twelve or so, and chased him, taking him to be a young thief or vandal.

But, on reaching the street outside, and even after running some way down it in both directions, he had been forced to return to the club. There had been no trace at all of any boy.

At the time of Monmouth's death and after reading the story he had given me, I confess that I was profoundly affected by it and by the events at the Club. But my own life was not touched any more closely, and so, inevitably, as the months and then years passed, the whole matter receded from my mind altogether.

Until very recently.

My business has prospered, I have become very well established. We remained in Norfolk while the children were growing up, though we also acquired a town house in Chelsea, but lately we have been looking at larger properties, in the home counties, and it was with some interest that I received particulars, from one of the house agents, of Pyre, Hisley Beeches, Berks. Indeed, after some searching, I managed to find Sir James's manuscript among the lumber in the attic, and in it to re-read the description of the house I knew we must certainly visit.

I felt strangely sad, driving down the avenue that Saturday afternoon, and the old man was much in my thoughts, the sight of him, in his familiar chair in the corner of the Club library, vivid before me.

The exterior of Pyre was exactly as he had described it, the park as it must have been then, and for the previous hundred years or more, and I felt my pulses racing at the thought, sentimental though it might be, that we might live here – I felt sure that it would have pleased him.

The interior, though, was quite ruined, ghastly in its vulgar, over-ornate furnishings and decorations – we went round it, seeing what amounted to the vandalism of what must once have been in such perfect restrained taste, and knowing that we could not conceivably be comfortable or easy here and that putting it all back to its original state would be a task quite beyond us. But we went on dutifully up the staircase, in and out of rooms with mounting horror as excrescences succeeded one another.

It was as we reached the end of a passage in the west wing that I saw the mirror. It was large, in a handsome gilded frame of considerably finer and more classic design than any of the other furnishings – so much so that I paused in some surprise, to admire it more closely.

And as I looked into the slightly foxed and pitted glass, the surface seemed to blur and dissolve, as if it were misting over with a fine white vapour. I stared in dawning recollection and fear, for the face that I saw staring back at me through the mist was not my own, but that of another.